BETWEEN THE DIMENSIONS

Sawyer saw three of the godlike Isier wading head and shoulders above the milling, battling figures, swinging great whips of flame that crackled and snapped like leashed lightning. A flung Sselli knife flashed toward one of the Isier—he smiled scornfully as it rang upon his ice-robed chest and fell harmlessly away.

And then, in a burst of shimmering heat, the strange figure of the Isier vanished. And Sawyer remembered: *When an Isier uses up more energy than he possesses, he seems to vaporize.*

The Isier drew their life-force from the Well of the Worlds, and in this final battle its energy was dwindling. . . .

HENRY KUTTNER

Novels

Available in Ace Books:

VALLEY OF THE FLAME (F-297)

EARTH'S LAST CITADEL (F-306)

THE DARK WORLD (F-327)

THE WELL
OF THE
WORLDS
HENRY KUTTNER

ACE BOOKS, INC.
1120 Avenue of the Americas
New York, N.Y. 10036

I

OUTSIDE the hotel window Clifford Sawyer could see the lights of Fortuna burning in the Pole's noonday darkness along all the plank paths of the little mining camp, glowing blue in the hospital windows, shining yellow in bunk houses and offices. He couldn't see the mine, of course, from here, but he could feel it. That deep, steady, almost subsensory *whump—whump—whump* had never stopped, day or night, for seventeen years now, since the mine was first opened in 1953. A great many people wanted uranium ore. The government needed its share, too, and the pumps never stopped, down under the frozen cap of the world.

Reflected in the glass, he saw the girl behind him stir impatiently. He turned his gaze back toward her, thinking that he had never seen eyes quite the shape and color of Klai Ford's. There was a touch of exoticism about her which he had been trying in vain to place, remembering what he had read yesterday in the files of the Royal Atomic Energy Commission, back in Toronto, about the curious background of this girl who had inherited half a uranium mine a few months ago.

She had smooth, caramel-colored hair. Her brow was bland and her eyes round, confiding and a singularly deep blue. Sawyer liked the way her front teeth stuck out ever so slightly, in an appealing sort of way that made him think of the ill-fated Lise Bolkonskaya in *War and Peace,* whose pretty little upper lip was too short for her teeth. The planes of Klai Ford's cheeks and the way the round eyes were set fascinated him. He had never seen just those structural lines before in any face on earth, and his experience had been wide.

Sawyer smiled at her. He had very white teeth in a very brown face, and his hair and eyes were a few shades lighter than his skin. About him was that relaxed air of alertness a man acquires who has reached a satisfactory compromise with life, and knows there will always be more compromises to make, as long as life lasts.

"I'll do my best," he told her, trying to place the curious little accent that had sounded in the girl's voice. "I don't even carry a gun, though. Our outfit usually works more with adding machines than with revolvers. Maybe you'd better tell me a little more. The Commissioner wouldn't have sent me up here if he hadn't figured I could solve your problem, in my own plodding way—which may be the best way to tackle—you said *ghosts?*"

"Yes, ghosts," the girl said firmly, and her odd little accent was as maddening as a tune you can't quite remember. "They're ruining our output. The miners won't even work some of the levels any more. Our refineries down south report the percentage of uranium in the pitchblends is dropping like *that.*"

She snapped her fingers and looked at him anxiously. "The mine *is* haunted. I'm not crazy, Mr. Sawyer, but I'm perfectly sure my partner would like you to think I am. That man's trying to close the mine. I think—" She clasped her hands tight and looked appealingly at Sawyer. "I know it sounds mad," she said, "but somebody's trying to kill me."

"Can you prove it?" Sawyer asked mildly.

"I can."

"Good. As for closing the mine, I don't think the Commissioner would allow it, so you needn't worry about—"

"He won't have any choice, if the uranium ore keeps

6

melting away," the girl interrupted. "After all, the government only manages the mines by courtesy these days. And Alper—" She paused, drew a long breath and met Sawyer's quiet gaze squarely.

"I'm afraid of him," she said. "He's a strange old man— half crazy, I think. He's up to something very odd. He's found something down in the mine. I should say he's found *someone*—" She broke off, laughing helplessly. "It doesn't make sense. But film doesn't lie, does it? What I've got on film, photographed in the mine, would be evidence, wouldn't it? That's why I sent for you, Mr. Sawyer. I want to put a stop to this before Alper and I go stark raving crazy together. There's a woman down in Level Eight—or the shadow of a woman. Oh, I know how it sounds! But I can show you."

"The ghost?" Sawyer inquired. He was watching her alertly, keeping his mind open or trying to. This wasn't the time to believe or disbelieve anything.

"No. *They* look like—" She hesitated, and then, oddly, said, "Wheat. They look like wheat."

"Wheat," Sawyer echoed thoughtfully. "I see." He paused. Then: "About this woman, though—you mean he meets one of the Fortuna women down in the mine?"

"Oh no. I know all the Fortuna women. Beasides, this isn't a real woman. You'll see what I mean in a minute. Alper's forbidden me to set foot in Level Eight, and the miners won't work there either; but he goes down and talks to this— this shadow of a woman, and when he comes back he—he frightens me. I'm afraid to go out alone any more. I take two men with me whenever I check the cameras in Level Eight. It seems idiotic to be so afraid of an old man like Alper, when he even has to walk with a cane, but—"

"No," Sawyer said carefully. "You're quite right about William Alper. He could be dangerous. We have a pretty complete file on him. In the old days he'd never have been allowed near this mine, you know. Owner or not. Luckily there are enough uranium sources now to let the owners have their whims, up to a point. But Alper's still on our list of potentially dangerous people. Partly because he's a very wealthy man, partly because he's an expert technician, and

7

partly, you know, because of that peculiar obsession of his about—rejuvenescence."

"I know." The girl nodded. "He's a strange man. I don't think he's ever failed at anything in his whole life. He's got an absolute conviction that he's the only man on earth who's always perfectly right about everything. He's determined the mine must close, and it drives him wild when I say no. Power's another obsession with him, Mr. Sawyer. He's imposed his will on so many people he must feel as basic as the law of gravity by now."

"He's getting old," Sawyer said. "He's getting panicky. Most people learn to compromise with age, but I doubt if Alper ever will."

"He isn't really as old as all that," Klai Ford said. "It's just that he's driven himself so hard all his life, as hard as he tries to drive others. Now he's beginning to pay for it and it makes him furious. I think he'd do anything in the world to get his youth back. He—he seems to think there may be a chance of it, Mr. Sawyer. That woman—that shadow—he meets in the mine seems to be playing on his obsession. She could talk him into doing anything at all. And she seems to want to get rid of me."

Sawyer regarded her with a steady gaze.

"This woman in the mine," he said, "leads me right into a personal question I've got to ask you, Miss Ford. A strange woman appearing from nowhere, right down there in the mine. Is that what you say is happening?"

All Klai Ford said was, "Oh, dear!" in a voice of misery.

"I've been trying to place your accent," Sawyer went on with calm relentlessness. "Would you mind telling me, Miss Ford, what country you come from?"

She jumped up abruptly, leaving the little nest of furs which was her thrown-back coat and hood. She paced up and down the room twice, then whirled.

"You know perfectly well!" she said accusingly. "Don't make it harder!"

Sawyer smiled and shook his head.

"I know, but I never really believed it," he said. "Naturally the Commission ordered a full investigation when you—ah—turned up here, but—"

"I don't know who I am!" the girl said angrily. "I don't know where I came from. Can I help it if I have a funny accent? I don't do it on purpose. How would you like to wake up with amnesia some morning and find yourself down in a uranium mine you'd never even heard of before, with no idea how you got there or who you were?" She hugged herself with both arms and shivered. "I hate it," she said. "But what can I do about it?"

"If you hadn't picked out a uranium mine to appear in—" Sawyer began.

"I didn't! It picked me!"

"—we wouldn't feel so baffled," Sawyer went on imperturbably. "I wish we hadn't tried so hard to find some explanation about you. Then at least we could say, 'Maybe there's some answer.' But we still know nothing whatever. I was wondering if any sort of answer has ever occurred to you."

She shook her head. "All I remember is waking up on the wet floor in the mine. I knew my name. Just one name—Klai. Old Sam Ford found me and took care of me, and finally adopted me when nobody could figure out where I came from." Her voice softened. "Sam was so good, Mr. Sawyer. And so lonely. It was he who made the strike up here, you know, back in '53. Alper financed it, but he almost never came to Fortuna, until after Sam died."

"Surely, Miss Ford," Sawyer suggested, "you've connected your own appearance in the mine with the appearance of this strange new woman? From the same place as yourself, do you think? Another woman, like you, who—"

"Oh, not a bit like me!" the girl said instantly. "*She's* one of the Isier, and they are gods!"

Then, as Sawyer stared at her, she clapped both hands over her mouth, gasped, and demanded, "Why did I say that? How did I know? Just for a second, I—I seemed to remember. That word I used—*Isier*. Does it mean anything? Is it English?"

"I never heard it. Try to remember."

"I can't." Klai shook her head wildly. "It's gone. I learned English after I came here, you know. I learned it in my sleep, mostly, from those hypnosis-tapes they have. But

9

surely the word couldn't have—no, I know it isn't English. It's part of my dreams. I—oh, this is nonsense! Let's get down to facts. I've got proof of a few things, anyhow."

She pushed up the sleeve of her blouse, uncovered a flat case taped to forearm, and grimaced as she tore the adhesive patch free. In her palm she held out a miniature case of ultra-small tape film.

"You have no idea what a lot of trouble I had getting this," she said. "I've got cameras hidden in Level Eight with all sorts of special shielding against radioactivity. Even that doesn't help when the—the ghosts come. They seem to be pure radiation. Anyhow the film goes black every time. But—well, just wait!"

She went efficiently across the room to unlock a cabinet and swing out a small film-projector. "Will you turn that picture over?" she said, nodding toward the opposite wall. "It's got a beaded screen on its back. I had everything ready, you see. This film's never been out of my hands since I took it from the camera. I did everything myself. Now I think you'll have real evidence to take back. Alper doesn't know a thing about this, thank goodness. I don't even want him to know I've talked to you, until I can prove enough to protect myself."

She clicked the switch. A square of pale light sprang across the room and flickered on the small screen. Dark, shadowy walls took shape upon the square, and a low throbbing came from the sound-projector, blending with the steady thumping of the great pumps themselves, under Fortuna.

As the pictured walls of the mineshaft flickered on the screen, Klai said suddenly, with a note of hysteria in her voice, "Mr. Sawyer, you haven't asked me a word about the ghosts."

"That's right," Sawyer said. "I haven't."

"Because you don't believe that part? It's true! They come *out of the rock.* I think that's why they're seen so seldom." She hurried on, frantic now. "Don't you see? How many shafts are there, compared to the *roads*—of pitchblende underneath? It's just accident when they blunder into a shaft, but the men do see them, like—like pale flames—"

10

Something like a pale flame flickered gently across the screen.

The girl laughed unsteadily.

"Not a ghost," she said. "A flashlight. Watch. Now it begins."

The flash-beam moved over rock, over jagged surfaces wet and shining and marked by the teeth of drills. Above the throbbing of the pumps a new sound came, the crunch of a cane among rubble and the noise of a man's heavy feet. Into the camera's range came a stooped, bulky figure, dimly seen. Sawyer breathed in with a sharp sound of recognition. The tiny square that flickered on the wall suddenly ceased to be a miniature reflection and seemed reality itself. He heard Alper's familiar, thick voice calling urgently.

"*Nethe!*" he said. "*Nethe!*" and the walls gave back the echoes until the whole tunnel was calling with him.

"Watch!" the girl whispered. "There to the left—see?"

It looked like a reflection upon the rock itself, except that the flash-beam did not touch it and there was nothing here to cast reflections. It looked like a tall woman, incredibly tall, incredibly slender, bending toward the half-seen Alper with an inhuman grace and flexibility. Now water dripped and tinkled, or—no, this was the laughter of a woman, pure silver, cold, inhuman as her motion.

A voice spoke, not Alper's. It was a voice like strong music. English was the language it used, but an English accented strangely—in the same way as Klai's, Sawyer realized suddenly. He slanted a glance at her, but she was watching the screen intently, her lips parted and her pretty teeth showing.

The voice was indistinct throughout the brief exchange of talk in the film. Echoes blurred it, laughter blurred it, and the woman seemed a shadow indeed, for she appeared to flicker now and then and her voice flickered with her.

Alper spoke. He sounded out of breath, and a desperate urgency was in his heavy voice.

"Nethe," he said. "Are you there?"

Laughter, like music, clear and rippling.

"Nethe, you're late! You're three days late. I'm running low. How long do you think I can last, without energy?"

The sweet, strong voice with music running through it said

11

carelessly, "Who cares how long you last, old man? Have you killed the girl for me?"

"I can't kill the girl," Alper's voice said angrily. The flash-beam danced across the rocks as he moved. "You don't understand. If I do it, *I'll* get into trouble, and who'll get the ore for you then? I might even lose the mine if she died. I've got a better way. I'm working on it. Any day now—"

"Who cares if a Khom dies?" the musical voice asked. "She's only a Khom. Worthless. Like you, old man. Why do I waste my time on you?"

"I tell you, I have a way! Give me a week. Give me energy to last and I'll have control of the mine. I'll close it, I promise I will! I'll find some way to close it down tight and hand it over to you. Only give me energy, Nethe! I tell you, I'm almost—"

"No," the voice of the shadow said. "No more. I'm tired of you, old Khom. I'll finish off the girl myself."

Alper lurched forward, obscuring the camera with his broad, hunched back. His cane scraped on the floor, his feet stumbled. Fierce despair was in his voice.

"I must have more energy!" he cried. The walls took up his words and the pitchblende itself seemed to be crying, "Energy! Energy!" out of the rock as if the mine were boasting of the potent power locked up there for the taking. "I must have more! Nethe!"

"No more," the shadow said carelessly. "Until you kill the girl."

"If you understood!" Alper said in a savage voice. "If you ever came up to the surface, you'd see what I mean. *Who are you, Nethe? What are you?*"

The cool, sweet, resonant laughter echoed among the rocks.

"Ask who I will be, three days from now," the shadow said. "Goddess! Goddess of— Oh, go back to your hovel, old man, and do what you please. But you get no more energy until you clear out the mine for me and kill the girl."

"No," Alper shouted. "Nethe, I've got to get more! I can't do anything without it! *Nethe!*"

The tall shadow bent toward him, inhumanly graceful, featureless in the gloom, laughing with a sound like water falling over rocks.

12

"Goodbye, old man," it said. "You'll get no more from me."

Alper stumbled forward toward the corner where the shadow flickered and faded. His desperate cry echoed down the endlessly repeating tunnel. His flash swept to and fro over the empty corner where a moment before the shadow of a woman had stood.

Then the film ran out. The picture died and a square of blank white shimmered on the wall.

Sawyer shook himself a little. For those brief few moments he had been standing in the tunnel, hearing the rocks drip and the pumps pound. The illusion had been so compelling that he was almost startled to realize that the hotel room still closed him in and that the girl called Klai was watching him with anxious blue eyes.

"Well?" she said impatiently. "What do you make of it?"

Sawyer gave her one of his alert, quick looks. Then he walked across to the window and gazed out upon the noonday bustle of Fortuna in the dark. He got out a cigarette, lit it, blew smoke at the glass.

"I'll tell you what I make of it. Not what you expect. I *don't* think some mysterious creature from beyond the veil has persuaded Alper to sell his soul. The film's very interesting, yes. The Commissioner will be fascinated by it. Faked or not, and you could have been deceived, Miss Ford, it's still very illuminating."

"I couldn't have been deceived," the girl said hotly. "I tell you, the film was never out of my hands. But—never mind that. Who is this Nethe? What do you think?"

"I think somebody's going to great pains to get control of the mine," Sawyer said. "That's obvious. There are countries that could use more uranium ore than they've got. This seems like a very ingenious little scheme to take advantage of an old man's obsession. It's high time we put a stop to it. Do you understand what Alper kept saying about energy?"

The girl shook her head.

"I don't understand anything. But I seem to remember—it's like a shutter opening and closing so fast all I get is a glimpse before the memory blacks out. But Nethe—" She shivered. "Nethe frightens me."

"This is the only thing you've filmed to date that shows

13

any clear pictures?" Sawyer asked. "I'd like to get back to Toronto with whatever you have. I do believe you're in danger. So is the mine. I want to start wheels turning to protect you. There seem to be all sorts of interesting possibilities."

"I've still got some film running off, down below," the girl told him. "Shall I get it?"

"I'd like to see what you have, but—isn't Level Eight a pretty dangerous place?"

"I never go alone," she said, turning to reach for her furs. Sawyer helped her into them dubiously.

"I'd better come along," he said. "I'd like to take a look at—"

The door jarred under the impact of a violent blow. Simultaneously a thick voice from the outside called, "Open the door!"

II

SAWYER MOVED with silent smoothness toward the projector. With a few deft motions he freed the little spool of film, slipped it into its case, and dropped the case itself in his pocket.

"It's Alper!" Klai said, darting panicky blue glances about the room. "He mustn't find me here! He mustn't know!"

Sawyer said, "Calm down," and took out his key-ring. "I have a passkey here. I never like to get locked into rooms with only one exit. That door over there gives into the next bedroom. I'll let you out. Wait for me. I don't want you to go down into the mine alone. Do you understand?"

"Yes, yes," she said, huddling her fur hood about her face. "Do hurry!"

Another tremendous thump upon the outer door made the windows rattle behind them.

"Sawyer!" the deep, thick voice from outside called imperiously. "Are you there?"

"Coming," Sawyer answered in a patient voice. In a whisper he added, "Out with you, now. And remember what I said."

He locked the door behind her scared departure, smiling

14

at the desperate scuttle with which she crossed the next room toward the exit. Then he went back leisurely and opened the door upon which a third great thump was still resounding.

"Come in, Alper," he said, mildly, politely, but his face tight with alert expectancy.

The man on the threshold filled the doorway from side to side. For a moment he stood there, leaning on his cane, peering up under his eyebrows. He was a troll, Sawyer thought. A thick, squat figure of an old giant who had bowed beneath his years until he could no longer move without his cane. The massive face sagged in deep pleats and folds. Two cold, small grey eyes looked up with singular dispassion at Sawyer under thick lids and thicker brows. A voice like a muffled organ said, "Do you remember me, Mr. Sawyer?"

He did not wait for an answer. He stumped forward and Sawyer fell back involuntarily. The man was so massive he seemed to push and compress the very air before him when he moved. The small eyes flickered once at the wall where the reversed picture hung.

"Get me a chair, Mr. Sawyer," Alper said, leaning on his cane. "It isn't easy for me to move around very freely. I'm an old man, Mr. Sawyer. Thank you." Heavily he lowered himself, leaned the cane against his knee. "I see you've been enjoying a very interesting film," he said, and watched Sawyer without emotion.

Sawyer said only, "Oh?"

"I watched too," Alper told him heavily. "Does that surprise you? This hotel was built in the old days when uranium was top-secret material. Sam Ford and I eavesdropped on many an important conference in this very room. Nothing, perhaps, quite as important as what's happening now." He blew out his breath and fixed Sawyer with a compelling gaze.

"I am here, Mr. Sawyer, to make you an offer."

Sawyer laughed gently.

"I was afraid you'd take that attitude," Alper said. "Let me go into the case more fully. I'm prepared to offer you—"

He spoke in detail for perhaps sixty seconds. At the end of it, Sawyer laughed again, very politely, shook his head and then waited, looking alert. Alper sighed his ponderous sigh.

"Young men are such fools," he said. "You can afford idealism now, maybe. When you get to my age, things look different." He seemed for some moments to consider a private matter. Finally he shook his heavy head. "Don't like to do it," he murmured. "Still—" He reached into the pocket of his rumpled coat and held something out on a large, unsteady palm. "Take it," he said. "Study it. What do you make of it?"

Sawyer rather gingerly accepted between thumb and forefinger a small, metallic, faceted disc about the size of an aspirin tablet. It was curved slightly on the underside. He looked up inquiringly.

"A little something of my own," Alper said complacently. "A transceiver, actually. It transmits sound and it receives sound. But a very specialized sort of sound. I don't know how familiar you may be with communication machines. One of the vital factors in any such device is the intensity of the internal noise of the receiving system. For instance, there is a constant sound and motion inside the human skull—the human body is such a communication machine. The heartbeat reverberates in it. The frictional whispering of blood moves through the arteries of the brain. The sound of breathing is loud in the passages of your head. Normally you are oblivious to these sounds. But they could be amplified."

Alper leaned back and smiled. There was, Sawyer thought, distaste and dislike in the smile. Perhaps an old man's jealous dislike of a young one.

"This device is such an amplifier," he said.

The thing vibrated slightly in Sawyer's hand, was still, vibrated again. Sawyer glanced at Alper's hand, which had gone back into his pocket.

"You're making it vibrate?" he asked. The old man nodded.

"And why," Sawyer asked politely, "are you showing this to me?"

"Frankly—" Alper said, and suddenly snorted with laughter. "Frankly, I may as well confess the truth. I made it for the head of Klai Ford. I am somewhat distressed to realize that you saw the humiliating part I played in that film. You saw me begging for something I most urgently need. You saw it—refused. Very well. You also heard my statement that I

16

had a method to bring Klai to heel. That wasn't idle boasting, Mr. Sawyer. This transceiver is the method."

Sawyer looked at him, puzzled and wary.

"I can trust you," Alper said sardonically. "More than you know. The one thing I won't risk is endangering my bargain with my—with the person I spoke to in the mine."

"Has she really got you convinced," Sawyer asked him, "that she's tapped the fountain of youth?"

"You fool!" Alper said with sudden violence. "What do you know about youth? Do you think *I* could be fooled by mumbo-jumbo? Where do you think the energy comes from that you young men squander? From the sun, through photosynthesis, turning into a form your body can accept as fuel! Some radiations you can get directly from the sun. And electric energy can be conducted from one person to another. You'll believe me—later.

"This is something a young man couldn't comprehend— Mephistopheles didn't bargain for Faust's soul. I *know*. It was Faust who had to convince the devil his soul was worth buying, in a buyer's market. And I had to convince Nethe I could be useful to her. I know what she demands in return for the energy I need. Klai's life depends on *me*, whether I can remove her as an obstacle so Nethe won't need to eliminate her. And I don't want Klai killed. The investigation afterward might be—awkward.

"So I made this transceiver. I worked it out myself, in private. I meant it for Klai, but I see now that could be even more of a nuisance than the girl. I came here today prepared for trouble." He laughed. "Here we go!" he said.

Alper was a ponderous man. He was also an old and a feeble man. What he did just now was therefore clearly impossible. He stood up straight. He pushed the cane violently away, so that it clattered to the floor besied his suddenly and strongly upright figure. The troll was still ponderous, but he was no longer stooped and feeble. A sort of impossible power flickered through him like a visible current. It was not youth, or muscular strength. It was something less natural, less explicable than suddenly restored physical power.

Sawyer heard the cane clatter without realizing what had

happened. He was a young and active man, but he was no match for this unnaturally violent old one. Alper's leap across the space that parted them was exactly the leap on an electric current between high-voltage terminals, not a physical body's motion propelled by muscular action. Muscular action seemed to have nothing to do with it. Alper's heavy bulk moved on some other propulsive force than muscle and bone.

The cane clattered. In the same instant the tremendous weight of that heavy old body hurtled against Sawyer's chest, drove him six feet backward and flattened him hard against the wall. A ponderous forearm jammed against his throat all but throttled him. The room swam blackly before him. Dimly he was aware that at the very crown of his skull some curious sudden pressure took place.

And then it was all over.

The pressure released him before he could gather himself to fight Alper off. When the first clatter of the cane had warned him, Sawyer's brain had sent a message to his body and his muscles flexed to respond. Alper's incredibly quick action took place in the split second needed for an active young man's reflexes to answer a summons to action. Sawyer thrust violently against the old man's bulk in the same instant that all power failed Alper.

It had been rapid. It was soon ended. But it had been enough.

Alper collapsed before Sawyer's thrust, helpless as a sack of flour. He fell heavily to the carpet, the floor shaking to the impact of his weight. He caught himself on one arm, wheezed noisily, and looked up under his thick, folded lids at Sawyer with a sly triumph on his empurpled face.

"Hand me my cane." he said.

Sawyer was massaging his throat with one hand and cautiously touching the crown of his head with the other. He paid no attention. Once the menace of Alper's weight was removed, he had a more immediate problem to solve. That strange, light, tingling area at the top of his skull. . . .

"Hand me my cane," Alper said again. "Sawyer! You may as well learn now to jump when I speak. You'll get used to it. *Now!*"

18

When he said *now*, thunder suddenly cracked Sawyer's skull wide open.

The shaft of it seemed to strike downward straight through his skull and into the middle of his brain. Through a haze of forked lightnings he saw Alper's grimly smiling face watching him. He clapped both hands to his head to keep the separating halves of his skull from falling entirely apart. While the thunder still crashed in his head he could do nothing at all but stand rigid, enduring it, holding his temples with both hands.

But it died at last. And then Sawyer whirled on the man at his feet, murderous anger flooding through his mind in the wake of the receding thunder.

"Careful!" Alper said in his thick voice. "Careful! Do you want it again? Now hand me my cane."

Sawyer drew a long, uneven breath.

"No," he said.

Alper sighed. "You're a useful man," he said. "I could kill you very easily. I could shake your brain to such a jelly you'd obey me, but if I did that, you'd be no use. To me or anyone. Be reasonable, Sawyer. I've got you. Why not co-operate. Would you rather die?"

"I'd rather kill you," Sawyer said, still pressing his head with both hands, and between them looking down with a grim defiance that matched the old troll's grim resolution. "I will, when I can."

"Ah, but you can't," Alper told him. "Shall I prove it again? Shall I prove you can't touch me fast enough to stop the—the lightning? You're behaving very stupidly, Sawyer. I want to talk to you, but I can't do it from the floor and I can't get up alone. I want my cane. I'll count three, Sawyer. If you haven't handed me my cane by then, you know what to expect. You'll have to learn the lesson, my boy."

Sawyer set his teeth. "No," he said, and braced himself for the instant thunder. He was not rational at this moment. His mind had been shaken clear down to bedrock by the inexplicable torment of the thunder, but the stubborn determination of the animal ruled him now—not to yield, though it killed him. He only knew that if he surrendered now he would be Alper's man forever, and no thunder, no pain, no cracking of the fibers of the mind could force him to that extremity.

"No," he said to Alper, and set himself for whatever might come.

"One," Alper said relentlessly.

"No."

"Two—" Alper said.

Sawyer grinned a fierce, mindless grimace, and without warning, even to himself, found himself launching at Alper's thick throat.

The thunder cracked his head wide open and lightning wiped the room out of existence. The last thing he saw was the floor pitching upward toward him.

When he could see again, Alper was half a dozen feet away, levering himself painfully towards his cane, breathing hard and watching Sawyer with bright, still eyes under the heavy lids.

"All right," Alper said. "You're quite a boy, Sawyer. I'll get the cane myself. Sit up. You're all right. I haven't damaged you permanently—yet. Get up and take a chair, my boy. You and I have some talking to do. And first of all, to be on the safe side, there's a matter of evidence that I intend to destroy." He glanced around the room. "That metal waste-basket should do nicely to burn a film. So—give me that film, Sawyer."

Sawyer said painfully, "Come and get it, you—"

Alper smiled.

A few final wisps of smoke rose from the waste-basket and faded. Sawyer, breathing a little hard, leaned back in his chair and stared at the old man. Curiously, now that the thunder had passed he felt no ill effects. He seemed perfectly normal. But his brain cringed at the thought of what Alper had just done to him—could do to him again, apparently at will. What was Alper saying now?

"You had better understand first exactly what has happened to you. Afterward you'll realize that you are going to do precisely as I say from now on, or you will die. I'm willing to go a long way with you, because you're a good man. You're better than I expected. I admire you. I respect you. But I'll kill you if I have to. Is that clear?"

20

"No," Sawyer said, lifting a tentative hand toward his head. "Do you really expect to get away with this?"

"I do," Alper said. "Go ahead, try to remove that transceiver. You can't without killing yourself. There are tantalum probes making contact with your brain itself, through the bregma—the opening at the vault that closes as a man ages. Luckily, you're still young enough to have a vestige of the fontanel still open. Luckily for me."

Sawyer lowered his investigatory hand. He still felt that if he could kill Alper he could stop the thunder, or at least die trying. But information might show him a better way, and Alper seemed quite willing to talk.

"Maybe I couldn't remove this thing," Sawyer said, "but I could get it removed."

"Possibly," Alper said. "There's a contact compression that will eventually form a semi-permanent ceramic-to-bone bonding, of course. But at present the tantalum probes as a nerve-contact serve the purpose. It's an amazing little device, isn't it?"

"Fascinating," Sawyer said grimly. "Who did you steal it from?"

Alper chuckled.

"I'm not a bad technician myself," he said. "Though I admit the original design wasn't my idea. I did make some improvements. I saw possibilities the inventor didn't. A miniature electrostrictive device like this—a transducer, let us say, which converts sound pressure to electric signals and back again—oh, I could see the possibilities very easily. It was simply a matter of applying the properties of light to the principles of sound. Sound, like light, can reflect, and can be amplified . . . Yes, my young friend—down through the bregma, into the cavities of your skull, reaches that transceiver to pick up sounds your senses are too dull to catch, and amplify them and reflect them back directly into the temporal lobe, the auditory area. And other brain-centers are involved too, as the wave-motions pass through motor and somesthetic areas. Implicit in your skull is the sound of the trumpets that shattered the walls of Jericho!"

He began to laugh. "You know what high frequency ultrasonics can do, don't you? Shatter glass. Burn wood. Shake a human mind apart, Mr. Sawyer! And you might also consider the wave-motions of the brain—the alpha and kappa waves—which I believe the transceiver can receive and amplify.

"The beauty of it is, you can't get away from it. It's in you, inherent in your blood and breath and thoughts. If you could stop it—you die. But no one else can hear it. It's subjective. And so is madness, my boy. This is a very special and literal version of madness. So I think, in the end, you'll do as I ask."

He watched Sawyer not without sympathy, smiling as he saw the younger man's hands close in a tight, primitive clench.

"One other thing," he said quickly. "No doubt you would like to kill me. Don't. It would sove nothing. You see, your body-field has a damping effect on the transceiver's operation, which I can alter by the—ah—volume control of this." He half drew from his pocket a small, flat metal case and thrust it back out of sight immediately. "If you tried to remove the transceiver, the farther it's moved from your body-field, the less the damping effect, and that would soon kill you. My body-field provides a supplementary damper, but it takes the combined effects of both fields to keep the acoustic level of the transceiver below your threshold of safety. So if you took this control device from me—or if I died—you would die in either case. We would meet in Hell in no time. Out of breath, startled, I expect, but mutual murderers, and not the devil himself could convict either of us of the other's death, they would happen so nearly at the same time."

The bloodhound smile was genial.

"It's a multi-purpose device, too. It also is clever enough to act as a microphone—and here is the receiver." He patted his pocket. "It isn't keyed to pick up the internalized sounds you find so uncomfortable; I made sure of that. But it does report to me, quite accurately, spoken conversations. So when you go down into the mine with Klai Ford soon and get the rest of the film she's planted down there, I'll be able to keep track of exactly what's happening. I don't expect there'll be anything on the film this time. Klai was miraculously lucky." He nodded at the waste-basket with its charred ashes.

"So," he said, with an air of finality, "you'll give me any further evidence you happen to run across. Meanwhile, you'll report by radio to headquarters that this—this affair seems to be a false alarm. As for Klai, the safest thing she could do is leave Fortuna. If we can prove she has hallucinations—delusions of persecution—a year's rest at some private sanitarium might be the best way to eliminate the risk of Nethe's killing her. And Nethe will, if Klai persists in sticking her head in the lion's mouth. Quite impersonally. Without malice. Nethe's disinterest in ordinary human problems is—awkward, sometimes."

"Who is she?" Sawyer asked.

Alper paused, frowned a little, and shook his head slowly, as though he were as puzzled as Sawyer.

"No questions," he said. "Action, now. I have the whip hand, and I intend to use it. If you got away from me, you might find a way to remove the transceiver from your head —what man has made, man can unmake, I suppose. But I warn you, Sawyer, that if you get out of my sight without permission, I can and will kill you. You can never get out of my hearing, with your—your built-in microphone. Now my energy's low. I used up too much of it, and I've got to get more. That means closing the mine, as Nethe wishes. I've got to keep my part of the bargain before she'll keep hers. So—"

His cool gaze studied Sawyer calculatingly.

"You're a young man," he said. "You want to live, don't you? Well, I repeat my previous offer. I expect you to say no. But my offer of a job for life, working for me, holds good at any time you care to accept it. What have you to say now, young man?"

"Nothing."

"Nothing at all?"

"I was sent up here to do a job," Sawyer said quietly. "Maybe I've failed. I've had failures before. Every man has."

"Not every man," Alper said, with a sudden flash of curious pride.

Sawyer shrugged slightly. "Okay," he said. "Put it this way. I don't mind failing when a job's too big for me. But if that happens I figure it's up to me to pass along the job to somebody good enough to handle it. Right now the Royal

Commission's depending on me to take care of what looked like a routine check-up. It isn't routine. And maybe I've already failed. But if I have, it's my responsibility to notify the Commissioner—"

"I'd be fascinated to know just how you intend to go about that little matter without getting yourself killed," Alper said, with an unpleasant grin. "If you're sensible, you could collect two salaries—and the one I'd pay you would be considerably more than what you earn from the Commission."

"It would have to be a damned high salary," Sawyer said, "to compensate for this—headgear!" He touched his head lightly.

"I can remove it," Alper said.

H waited for Sawyer's reaction, seemed disappointed, and went on:

"I would even feel safe in removing it, under certain circumstances. Who would believe your story? But first, I'd make perfectly certain that you intended to remain cooperative."

Sawyer said thoughtfully, "How could you remove the transceiver? You said it had a ceramic-bone seal to my skull, didn't you?"

"Not yet—not for weeks. Until then, I can turn off the power entirely, and if I do that—and only if I do that—can you lift the transceiver from your head without committing suicide. Yes, I can turn off the power. There is a way. The secret is here, in the control case in my pocket—but I spent more time devising that shut-off switch than I spent on the rest of the work combined. So don't waste time hoping you could find the way to turn off the power-switch, by examining my control case. Houdini couldn't find the way, and it would take a differential analyzer to find the—ah—combination. So I think you understand that you'll do what I tell you. Yes, you'll do that, my boy," and here Alper smiled ferociously, "or you'll die."

They were looking at each other with a measuring stare, each waiting for the other to make a definitive move, when from outside a sudden earsplitting din made the windows rattle.

Both men wheeled toward the sound. A siren screamed its

24

high, shuddering wail for three piercing beats and then subsided. A voice, amplified to hollow impersonality, spoke tremendously through the darkness of Fortuna's noon.

"Trouble in Level Eight!" the voice informed the little city and the cold, still night of the Pole. "Trouble in Level Eight!"

Alper turned snarling to the younger man.

"The little fool!" he said. "She went down! After all my warnings, Klai went down, and now Nethe's got her!"

III

LIKE A MAN in a dream, Sawyer followed Alper's stumping, fur-swathed figure through the turmoil of Fortuna toward the mine. In the distance he could see the bare, windswept ice of Little Slave Lake giving back reflections from the eternally lighted town. Fortuna was set down like a small medallion of humanity on the vast curve of the globe, clasped to it as the transceiver was clasped to Sawyer's skull, and as alien to the rock as the transceiver to the head.

They stumbled and slipped on icy planks as they made their way toward the mine. Fortuna had no streets. Plank steps and runways linked the buildings, which were anchored tight to the bedrock of the planet itself, for there was no soil here. Nothing grew except Fortuna. No roads led into it. The silence of the world's end seemed to close it in. Whenever human noises faltered here, the vast silence of the Barrens closed over them like water.

Slipping on ice, breathing the dry, incredible cold, Sawyer followed the stumping Alper. Out of bunk houses, offices, shack-like private homes, curious crowds were flocking. Alper thrust them aside, answering no questions. They passed the lighted commissary, the cook-house, the powerhouse, hearing the huge diesels that generated the lifeblood of Fortuna, lighted the houses, drove the mine machinery, pumped the waters of Little Slave Lake continually and forever out of the shafts where continually and forever they seeped.

They passed the last of the ugly, utilitarian buildings which two hundred people needed for their encysted life above the pitchblende veins. And they came at last to the mouth of the great mine.

Alper shouldered through the excited knot around the entrance. The voice had ceased to echo its alarm-signal from amplifiers spaced under eaves all along the streets, but other voices had taken it up now, a babble of them, excitedly predicting disaster.

"The ghosts are loose!" Sawyer heard one miner say to another. "Down in Eight they're busting through the walls!"

"Miss Ford's down there," someone else volunteered as Alper passed. "The ghosts have got Miss Ford!"

Alper shrugged them off. He had one purpose now and one only, and his strength was visibly lagging. Sawyer, following him into the lift, thought with grim amusement that at any rate, for the moment, they had one goal in common—neither wanted Klai Ford to die.

There was always pandemonium underground at Fortuna. The noise of drills, carts, automatic muckers never ceased. Men's voices echoed and re-echoed endlessly. It was a disorderly pandemonium now. All work seemed to have come to a full stop, and shouts from below made hollow reverberations that rebounded among the shafts. The lift passed opening after opening that swarmed with grimy faces with lights burning above every forehead. Abandoned drills and shovels leaned against the walls where shining ribbons of pitchblende showed the marks of labor, steel-hard stuff, heavy as lead and rich with uranium as a pudding with plums. Rich, that is, Sawyer thought, unless the ghosts have been at it. . . .

"They're swarming like bees in Level Eight!" someone called warningly as the descending men passed. Alper only grunted. He had taken Sawyer's arm as they stepped into the elevator, and now his weight was heavy against the younger man. As the mechanism ground toward a halt, he muttered thickly, his breath coming in uneven gusts:

"Don't—try anything. I warn you, Sawyer. Got to help me. Used up too much back there. My last energy—"

"What you were saving to put this gimmick on Miss Ford?" Sawyer asked. "You made a mistake, Alper. If any harm comes to her, the government's going to ask some pretty close questions. Killing me won't help. It won't save you."

"Let me handle this," Alper wheezed. "Do as you're told. Come on."

They stepped out into the mouth of Level Eight, into a cluster of pale, excited men. Voices echoed dully here and the air felt thick and heavy, pressing upon the ears. Sawyer noticed an unexpected smell of—ozone?

"She went in there," one of the men at the shaft-mouth said, turning his helmet-light toward them as the two stepped out of the lift, Alper's heavy weight sagging on Sawyer's arm. "Here's Joe, Mr. Alper. He was with her."

"What happened?" Sawyer asked crisply. The miners' troubled, frightened faces swung round toward him, their lights moving in flickers across the wet walls. One of them stepped forward.

"Miss Ford had Eddie and me come down with her," he said. "She waited right here. Nobody else was around. We don't work Level Eight any more, because—well, we don't work it. Miss Ford sent Eddie in to get a camera she wanted."

A murmur from behind him made everyone look up. The tunnel twisted out of sight into the rock ten feet away. From beyond the bend, a faint flicker of light showed, faded, showed again. The air seemed to ring soundlessly, as if bells were swinging far away, sending out sound-waves that compressed the inner ear. The smell of ozone grew stronger.

"Go on," Alper grunted, shuffling forward. "Go on, I'm listening." The miners made way for him. Sawyer let the grip on his arm pull him on. He was very alert, every sense straining for impressions.

"Eddie got just around that bend, out of sight," the miner told them. "Excuse me, Mr. Alper—I don't feel like coming any farther." He stood back stubbornly. "I'll finish in a minute. There isn't much to tell. Eddie started yelling. Then the ghosts came— Anyhow, we saw those lights begin to flash and Eddie yelled. Miss Ford said for me to come. She said we had to get the camera. We—well, she got ahead of me. And Eddie let out one awful scream and stopped, and— Miss Ford was around the bend, and I—I came back fast to set off the alarm." The man's voice was guiltily defiant.

"Did Miss Ford scream?" Sawyer asked.

27

"No sir. Not a sound."

Alper grunted again and lurched forward, toward the darkness and the flickering of unearthly lights around the bend of the tunnel. It was very silent there. The underground had swallowed up Klai Ford and the man named Eddie, and only the flicker seemed alive in there now. The miners' faces, scared and awed, watched the two men around the bend and out of sight. No one made a move to follow.

"Sawyer!" Alper wheezed, leaning heavily against him as they made their slow way forward. "Let me handle this. Don't make any moves on your own. I'll stop you if I have to. Understand? I've got my hand on the control of the transceiver right this minute. One touch and I could kill you in your tracks. I think Nethe has got the girl. I want to keep her alive if I can, but—"

He didn't finish. He didn't need to. It was obvious that Nethe, with her mysterious energy-source, would survive if it came to a choice. Sawyer knew that the choice must not be left to Alper.

They came to the first bend in the tunnel. A flicker of lights fled away from them between walls of shining rock around the next bend. Stubbornly Alper shuffled on, Sawyer supporting him. The smell of ozone was heady in the air. . . .

Then they saw the ghosts.

A dead man lay prone on the wet floor of the tunnel just around the next bend. And swarming over his body, dancing, flickering, rising and falling in the air, a whirl of winged lights shimmered. It seemed to Sawyer that suddenly wide spaces had opened all around him. The indigo smell of ozone was sharp in his nostrils; he had a feeling of breathless delimitation, and an intangible wind roared soundlessly through the tunnel.

The whirl of wings above the dead man were split flames, two by two, joined at the base in a V. Wheat-shaped, Klai had said. Like pale grain, dividing at the top into a fork of flickering light. The air seethed with them; flat, thin, dancing things shivering into fringes of light at the edges. They were beautiful. They were terrifying. They danced like vultures over the dead man, dipping, wheeling, with a dread-

28

ful eagerness stooping toward him and whirling high again. The whole tunnel dazzled with their motion.

Alper paused. Sawyer felt a tremor of some violent emotion shake the ponderous body that leaned against him. Then in a suddenly thin voice the old man called aloud:

"Nethe? Nethe, are you here?"

A familiar ripple of laughter sounded out of the darkness beyond the dancing wings of fire. It was the only answer, but when Alper heard it he drew a deep breath and shuffled forward resolutely, keeping his face turned toward the wings of light.

Sawyer asked softly, "What are they? Do you know? Did *they* kill the man?"

"I don't know. I don't care," Alper said. "Hurry. All I do know is Nethe's there and I can get energy again. Youth again! Hurry!"

Sawyer hesitated. He thought, "Is this my chance? If he gets more energy it may be too late, but now, while he still wants something of me—"

Without completing the thought, he sprang into sudden, violent action, leaping back away from Alper and the flames, disengaging his arm from Alper's weight and clearing his own right hand for the quick sidewise blow that would free him, if he were lucky, from the tyranny of the old man's power.

"Last chance," he told himself as he sprang. "Maybe he was lying. Maybe not. Maybe if he's knocked out I can get the transceiver control away from him. Maybe—"

Thunder and lightning crashed downward again in the familiar path through the center of his head. The tunnel wheeled dizzily, flashing with lights that were not all the winged ghosts. Alper's heavy hand shut around Sawyer's wrist before his brain cleared.

"Come on! Hurry! Don't make me do it again! There isn't time!"

Staggering and dazed, Sawyer let himself be pulled forward. The winged flames seemed to consider them as they stumbled past, to flutter a little and then subside again as if in some radiant feast upon the dead man on the floor. Shuddering and dizzy, Sawyer accepted the old man's weight once more, let himself be urged on into the darkness beyond the flames.

Before them the shaft widened. There was light again, a broad circle of it upon the wall, like the light of a distant flashbeam, pale and wide. Flattened against the light, Klai stood motionless, pressing her back to the rock and staring straight before her into the shadows.

Sawyer stared, shook his head and stared again. The light came from *behind* the girl. It fell through the solid rock, from some point beyond. Klai was motionless, her head thrown back, her palms flat against the wall, and suddenly Sawyer realized that her immobility was deceptive, no choice of hers. For she was trying frantically to move.

And she could not. Like a moth pinned upon the circle of light she stood, fought hard and could not stir a finger. Only her quick breath and the flash of her eyes and the glint of her white teeth beneath the pretty upper lip as she spoke showed that she was alive at all. Her voice sounded frantic.

"You can't do this!" she cried into the shadows. "You're not allowed to! You're not the Goddess!"

Automatically Sawyer turned his head to follow her gaze. In the darkness a luminous shadow stirred. Nethe was a preternaturally tall figure clothed in shadows, holding them about her like a veil through which her face gleamed dimly. Try as he would, Sawyer could not focus upon the figure and the features under the veil. But the voice was clear, very strong and sweet, with such music latent in it as an angel might hold latent, not choosing to release the full volume in a world so limited as Earth.

"I will be Goddess, soon enough," Nethe said. "How do you know me, Khom? You *are* a Khom! A real Khom, not an earthling. How did you get here, girl?"

"I don't know. I don't know!" Klai's voice wavered. "But you're not the Goddess. You can't be, without the Double Mask. Oh, I wish I could remember—"

Nethe's voice broke in sharply, in a language full of curious double consonants that lisped like diphthongs. Her words crackled. Klai caught her breath in a sound like a sob.

"I don't understand you! I don't remember! Who are you? Why—"

30

Alper's forward lurch cut off the words. From the corner of her eye she saw the motion, gasped, and tried in vain to turn her head.

"Nethe—" Alper said.

Klai's blue eyes rolled sidewise. "Who is it? Alper, is it you?"

"Be still, Klai," the old man said. "If you want to live, be quiet."

"Why should the life of a Khom matter?" Nethe asked derisively. "Even to a Khom? I'm finished with you now, old Khom. I have the girl!"

"Don't do it, Nethe!" Alper's voice was desperate. "I'll lose the mine if you kill her! Then you won't get the ore at all."

"Your little Khom troubles are so important to you Khom," Nethe said. "But not really important at all."

"Her body will be found!" Alper cried. "They'll get me for murdering her! Nethe, you can't do it!"

"Body?" Nethe said contemptuously. "The body won't be *here*. I must question this girl before she dies. She is a Khom. If I had known that before—but how could I? All you animals look so much alike, and the girl spoke your tongue until just now, when I was about to kill her. Well, by doing that she's gained herself a reprieve—until she tells me how she passed through the Gate. I must understand that. But I had not intended . . . oh, it doesn't matter. I know a way— a safe place to question this Khom. And this time I may never need to return to your bleak world. So—goodbye, old Khom."

The willowy, bending figure swooped forward, trailing shadows. Out of the veils one arm suddenly thrust, incredibly long, incredibly graceful. Between finger and thumb a sudden brilliance sprang out. She held what looked like a little golden bar six inches long. She seemed to press it and it split into wheat-shaped wings, a tiny duplicate of the ghosts behind them in the passage. The wings unfurled golden fire, shot out brilliance that dazzled the eye. Holding the thing high before her, she swept forward toward Klai. And as she neared the wall, the circle of light grew brighter and brighter.

Alper's caught breath seemed to strangle him. The instant the shining thing sparked in Nethe's hand he had seemed to

31

galvanize into a sudden convulsion of excitement. He thrust Sawyer away with what must have been his last remaining dregs of energy, and lurched forward upon Nethe like a man magnetized by what he saw, helpless to hold back from it.

"Give it to me, Nethe!" he cried in a hollow voice, reaching out both hands. "Nethe, let me have it! Let me touch it once more! Nethe, I—"

Sawyer, seeing the old man's hand out of that fatal pocket, leaped past him like a spring released. He didn't know what he hoped to accomplish, but Nethe seemed the obvious antagonist just now and he thought, with one stroke of clarity in his otherwise confused brain, that if he could snatch the sparkling wings out of her hand he might hold the key to more than it was possible yet to understand.

Everything happened with dazzling suddenness.

His outstretched arms closed about the tall, shadow-veiled figure in the instant before Alper reached her. Under the veil he felt a body preternaturally slender, impossibly lithe, very hard and stronger than a steel cable. Shocked and startled by the feel of it, he hung on hard. He had hoped to control her with one arm while he reached for the shining thing, but this was like trying to hold the Midgard Serpent.

He heard her scream—one wild, furious, ringing cry like a struck gong, resonant with music and incandescent with rage. The steel cable of her body sprang to violent life, lashing like a snake in his arms. He knew he could not hold her. But he could hang on for a moment. Gasping, shocked into witlessness, he clasped that writhing column—

Alper shouted, a strangled cry. Past Sawyer's face something bright flashed sparkling toward the floor. Alper swooped, snatching it in midair, lunging against Sawyer as he did so. The impact struck Sawyer off balance, and Nethe whirled out of his arms like a tornado swaying sidewise.

Alper was a man transfigured. The sparkling thing seemed to bathe him in radiance, and the years dropped visibly from him as he stood there clutching it. The sag of his body straightened, his heavy cheeks grew firm, his eyes glowed with fanatical triumph. He whirled like a young man, strong and quick.

32

"So this was it!" he cried. "*This* was where the energy came from!"

"Give it back to me!" Nethe screamed, swooping forward. "You don't know what you're doing! You can get too much energy, old Khom. Look, the Gate's beginning to open! Give it back!"

Alper whirled away for her, laughing drunkenly. Sawyer could see now that it was not youth that had transfigured him. The old face was old still, but firm with an unnatural firmness. The old body was still heavy and thick, but energy seemed to pour through it in a golden torrent.

Nethe swooped and snatched with both hands for the sparkling thing. Alper, spinning to elude her, struck the wall a violent blow with the bright opened wings. There was a ring of wild music, as if the rock had been an answering gong, and the circle of light grew too bright to look at. Klai was a shadow in silhouette against that brilliance.

"Close it, Alper!" Nethe screamed in the dazzle. "We'll all be drawn through! Alper! Close the Firebird! Keep it but *close it!*"

The air was ringing all around them. The circle of light was a tunnel's mouth, round, glowing, and leading down a long, diminishing circular hallway carved out of ice. . . .

A current seemed to catch them all and whirl them toward the tunnel. Nethe's cry of rage and despair made the ice-walls ring. There was a humming and a whistling in the air, and a sudden storm of light-wings beat about their ears. The wheat-shaped flames from the tunnel were fluttering past, flattening themselves upon the tunnel walls, glittering and fading. . . .

Alper, with belated terror, snapped the golden thing in his hands shut. But it was too late. The current had them. They were whirling and falling, and walls of ice spun by endlessly around and around their flight. . . .

33

IV

THERE WAS an instant of such cold that Sawyer felt as if all the molecules of his body were shrinking together and clashing like crystals. Then he stood firm on a solid floor, gazing before him down a long, circular tunnel pale green like ice. He was not alone, for Klai was at his side, her knees sagging a little, and Alper stood three paces beyond, one hand against the ice-like wall and the other still clenched tight around the precious thing he held.

These weren't important. The thing that riveted the eye was the scattered throng of other figures, as far as Sawyer could see, gliding swiftly away from them down the tunnel. All of them were tall people, inhumanly willowy, and all of them seemed to be walking *backward*. Blank, blind faces smiled palely behind them as they walked.

Sawyer glanced at Klai. Her eyes were round and dazed and questioning. He looked at Alper, and met the same look of dazed bewilderment there. Tentatively Sawyer spoke.

"Alper," he said. "Can you hear me?"

His voice echoed hollowly down the hall. Alper tried twice before he could get the words out.

"Yes, I hear you. Where—"

"Where are we?" Sawyer asked in the same breath, echoing the same question. The younger man grinned bleakly, and Alper seemed to pull himself together with a strong effort, straightened, looked down at his own heavy body and laughed suddenly, a sound thick with triumph. Moving with powerful ease, he stepped away from the wall of green ice, solid and opaque behind them. On the other side of it, did the mine and Fortuna lie?

"I don't know where we are," Alper said. "But I know how we got here. *This*." He unclosed his hand and the golden bar caught the light of the tunnel and gleamed softly. Alper's thick fingers pressed it. Flat gold wings opened in a sparkling V and fringes of fire sprang out of them. Alper grinned and slapped the gold-winged symbol flat against the ice. It rang faintly and sweetly.

34

Nothing else happened.

Alper grunted with dismay, drew his arm back and slapped the thing again upon the ice. Still nothing, though a glow seemed to be growing in the air around them.

"Close it! Alper, close it!"

All of them turned. And for the first time, clearly, without her veil of shadow, they saw the woman called Nethe.

Among all those oblivious, drifting figures that receded from them down the corridor of ice, one alone seemed really animate. The rest moved like people in a trance. But one turned his head and looked at them blazingly over its shoulder from thirty feet down the hall. The motion made suddenly clear the mystery of all those blank, backward-staring faces.

The faces were masks. The real faces of the trance-gripped people fronted forward. But Janus-like at the backs of their heads, the masks stared blind-eyed and smiling. Only Nethe twisted frantically, as if in the grip of some irresistible forward flow, trying to look back.

They saw her face. A strange, inhuman face, brilliant with more than human vitality. It was narrow, pointed at the chin, widening toward enormous, lustrous, snake-like eyes half-veiled under heavy lids. Her mouth was a thin crimson crescent, curving upward like one of the half-mad smiles the early Etruscans carved upon their marble statues.

Her body, like the bodies of the dreaming shapes she moved among, was no more human than a figure by El Greco, and no less human. All of them had the slender, oddly spiraling distortion of height which El Greco gave his people. And like them, the elongated lines lent a curious grace and rightness to her body which made humanity seem warped and wrong by contrast.

She too wore one of the pale, smiling masks upon the back of her head, turned in profile as she twisted to look back. If she had hair you could not see it. Across the crown of her head, dividing mask and face, a glass crown ran in undulant loops. At her ears hung earrings like tiny perforated spheres inside which a gentle light glowed softly. Every motion sent points of patterned glitter moving across her cheeks as the earrings swung.

35

She was dressed like all the others of her kind here, in a flowing garment the color of pale green ice, sweeping free from a broad flat collar like a surplice. And she was struggling frantically to turn.

"Close it!" she cried again. "Quick! You can't go back that way!"

Now the air was shivering more violently. Sawyer said, "Shut it, Alper," and tried to turn and step back the three paces that parted them.

He could not do it.

Firmly, inexorably, the air resisted him. Not with a solid pressure, but more as if a stream of tiny, tingling points flowed constantly out of the wall behind them.

"I've been trying, too," Klai said quietly. "You can't. You can't even stand still. Look, we're starting to move."

Stumbling against the increasing pressure, Sawyer fought briefly and in vain. Ahead of them Nethe was struggling too, frantically, her strange face dazzling with anger and—was it anxiety? The current swept her and the figures like her as if on a strong, smooth breeze that flowed fast. Distance was already widening between them as she stretched out a demanding hand and called:

"Alper! Come to me! You have the Firebird, so you can move. Give it back!"

Alper laughed, an intoxicated sound. He had snapped the glitering wings shut and the air was quiet again, the light gone. He held the Firebird up derisively.

"You've doled me out my last measure!" he shouted to the receding Nethe. "Now I'll get it from the source! You fool, why should I give it up now?"

"I need it!" Nethe called despairingly. "You don't know what you're doing! What does your little Khom life matter, compared to mine! I don't dare go out, without the Firebird!" Her voice grew threatening. "Do you think when we come to the end of this passage I won't kill you and take it back? Hurry, Khom, hurry!" Already her voice was growing hollow with the echoes that reverberated from the walls of ice as distance drew out between them.

"Give it back!" she cried, from far away, a small, diminishing figure with blazing eyes. "Give it back and I'll let you live! But hurry, hurry, before I—"

One of the swiftly receding figures among which she moved swerved sidewise and brushed her shoulder jarringly. She twisted her head to look forward, and her wild, high cry of anger and despair made all the echoes ring. Those blank-faced, receding replicas of herself seemed to pay no attention to anything that was happening around them, not even to the echoes of Nethe's scream, but the increasing speed that swept them all along was swirling them now together toward a slow ripple of motion that closed off the far end of the tunnel.

Pale, ice-colored curtains swayed continuously there, like the aurora borealis, Sawyer thought—the same folds, the same motion. And between those folds, by ones and twos, the gliding figures were sweeping out of sight into some unguessable world beyond the tunnel.

"Alper!" Nethe's strong, singing cry made the echoes roll like music. "Alper, it's too late! Listen to me! Listen very carefully! They've seen me from outside by now. The Goddess will be waiting to trap me. I'll get to you if I can, but *hide the Firebird!* Show it to no one! If you want to live, keep it hidden until I come for you. Don't—"

A sudden wall of silence cut her voice off sharply. Nethe had vanished between the rippling curtains, straining her face around toward them to the last, the great, baleful eyes burning with urgency.

Alper shut his hand nervously over the closed Firebird, rubbed his face with a heavy hand, and looked doubtfully at Klai.

"I—I don't understand," he said. "Are we dreaming? Where are we? Klai, she seemed to think you—*do* you know what's happening?"

Klai held tighter to Sawyer's arm. The two of them were walking forward slowly now, under the gentle, irresistible pressure of the air. Alper took two or three quick steps to catch up with them.

"It isn't a dream," Klai said hesitantly, her strange accent oddly thicker than before. "It's more as if I'd dreamed about Fortuna and the Pole. I'm only beginning to wake

37

again now to the real world. My world—at the end of this hall. Khom'ad, where my people live. Where the—the Isier rule. Where—"

She broke off quite suddenly, catching her breath with a sharp gasp. Her fingers dug into Sawyer's arm in a convulsion of unexpected terror.

"Oh no!" she cried. "Oh, I can't go on! I can't go back." She tried frantically to whirl and retrace her steps. The furs she wore impeded her and her boots got no traction on the floor. She kicked them off and in sandaled feet made the most furious efforts to move against that forward-flowing current. But she made no headway at all.

"What is it?" Sawyer asked. "Tell us what you remember, Klai. What are you afraid of?"

"N-Nethe," Klai said. She turned quickly, with a shiver, toward those slowly approaching curtains beyond which the robed figures were still vanishing, blank mask-faces turned backward, to watch them with unseeing stares. "I remember —the Isier. When my grandfather was a temple slave, Nethe was already the Goddess-elect. The next priestess in line to wear the Double mask if the Goddess had to give it up. I've been away—" Here she touched her cheek wonderingly, as if her own body were as strange to her as these new-found memories.

"I've been away for two whole years, unless time runs differently on Earth. I had to leave. I can't go back! I was a chosen sacrifice to feed the Firebirds! What shall I do?"

She flashed a wild, pale glance up at Sawyer.

"Wait," he said. "Let's get this clear. At the far end of this tunnel you think—there's another world, is that it? Your world?"

"Think?" she echoed desperately. "I know! You saw Nethe. You see these others, these Isier. Do you imagine you're still in your own world? Do they look like people from Earth? Of course I know!"

Sawyer looked down at her thoughtfully. He looked at the blank-faced, receding masks, the tall, distorted figures sweeping forward above their own reflections in the shining floor. With a great effort he turned his head to look back at the closed wall they had come through. He wondered if someone had struck him over the head in the mine, and left him lying there on the wet floor dreaming feverish dreams.

"Dream or not," he said, "we'd better face it. Alper, you can move against this current. See if you can stop us."

Ponderously Alper swung his huge body before them in a reluctant effort. The smooth air-pressure carried them on, and himself with them, as easily as if he had not tried at all. Stepping aside, he took Klai's wrist in a firm grip and braced his heavy legs. Her forward motion carried him along without a pause, his feet sliding on the ice-like floor.

Sawyer sighed. "Well, it was worth trying. What comes next, Klai? What's out there beyond those curtains?"

"The city," she said impatiently, still making futile, scrambling tries to resist the forward flowing air. "Khom'ad, my world. Oh, there's so much to remember! It's all hazy, even now. I know this much—Nethe's dangerous!"

"Tell us what you remember about her," Sawyer said. "Quick! There may not be much time."

"She's an Isier, an immortal, one of the race of gods who rule Khom'ad.

"They never grow old. Nothing can hurt them. Even the Goddess would rule forever, unless trouble came and her people blamed her for it."

"Goddess?" Sawyer asked.

"Not really. Just an Isier like Nethe, only with great powers, and wearing the Double Mask and the Dark Robe. As Nethe will in three days, if she wasn't lying. I wonder! In the time I've been gone, the troubles must have got worse in Khom'ad or Nethe couldn't hope for a change of Goddesses."

"Troubles?" Sawyer prompted. "Anything that will affect us when we come out? Tell me what you remember."

"Trouble among the gods," Klai said uncertainly. "How could we Khom know the reasons? But the Isier had begun to—to vanish like mist sometimes, and nobody knew why. And there were strange, ugly, frightening people who came up from the world below, and not even the Isier could kill them. Mostly, for the Khom, the trouble meant sacrifices, though. Many sacrifices. Far more than the Isier ever used to need. They'll take me for an accepted sacrifice when we come

39

to the end of this place, and I'll go to feed the Firebirds in the next ceremony—"

"Maybe not," Sawyer said. "There may be some other way. Tell us what the Firebirds are. Like that thing Alper has?"

She shook her head in confusion. "You saw the Firebirds. The ghosts. The flying things that take the uranium out of pitchblende. That was something new to me. In Khom'ad we knew nothing of the Firebirds—only that deep down in the Well of the Worlds, where the sacrifices are thrown, sometimes a flicker of wings moves. That's why the Isier call it the Firebird Well, and the sacrifices feed the Firebirds. But in Khom'ad we never saw a real, living thing like those ghosts in the mine. Of course we didn't know about uranium, either."

She paused. "How strange it seems. Double memories all down the line. Everything double—Earth and Khom'ad."

"And this thing?" Alper asked, holding up his hand with the gold bar.

"I don't know. Nethe called it the Firebird. I suppose it's a symbol, a talisman. Opened, it looks like them, doesn't it? And it seemed to—summon them, did you think? You saw how the air shook and grew brighter when you held its wings open."

"It opened the wall when we came through," Alper said. "I know that—I saw it. But it seems to open one way only."

"A key?" Klai asked uncertainly. "Between worlds? I wonder if that's why Nethe wants it so badly. I'll tell you this much—if she's to be Goddess in three days, the Isier who's Goddess now will try to kill her. She won't give up the Double Mask without a struggle. Nethe will need that Firebird, if there's any power in it—to help her."

"There's power," Alper said in his thick, deep voice. "And I'll keep it. If Nethe wants anything from me, she'll have to—"

"Oh, you idiot," Klai said wearily. "Nethe's an Isier, a demigod. In my world you'll be nothing but a human being, one of the Khom. Don't you understand?"

Sawyer grinned suddenly. "You've been supping with the devil, Alper, you old Khom," he said. "Now it looks like a

40

damned short spoon you're holding. Look here. We may need what help we can give each other. You've got to release me from this thing—this transceiver. It may be your only weapon against Nethe, if you could use it on her. But once you step out of this hall you're at her mercy. You'll need any help you can get."

"No," Alper said heavily, his small eyes glinting with suspicion. "I'm free here. I don't have to leave the hall, the way you do. I'll just keep the whiphand I've got over you and see what happens."

Sawyer glanced at the curtains which rippled across the corridor's end, very near them now. Faster and faster the smooth-flowing air swept them forward.

"Like the flow of electrons in a vacuum tube," Sawyer thought suddenly, seeing the curtains sweep toward him. "You can't move against the flow, if you happen to be an electron. This end of the tunnel's the cathode, and—here we go!"

The curtains brushed their faces blindingly. The current of air blew them with final, gentle violence against the cathode. Then they stood blinking at the head of a broad, low flight of steps above an open square, with a stormy sunset lighting the sky above them. Sawyer's knees felt unsteady. The current had released them and they were dizzyingly free to stand alone.

"This is it," Klai said softly at his side. He heard the long unsteady breath she drew. "This is Khom'ad. And I'm back again. I'm—home."

V

IT WAS a noisy world. The steps led down to the crowded square, where the tall Isier, robed in flowing ice, moved majestically among swarms of the lesser breed called human. One of the Isier was playing a strange square drum, beating a wildly rhythmic tune, and a group of the gods around him swayed to the beat, their blank mask-faces turned outward.

Another knot of the double-faced people, vividly alive, argued fiercely over some sort of game at the foot of the steps,

41

a singing note in their voices even as they brawled. One of the entranced newcomers paused below Sawyer on the steps, shook his masked head dizzily, then gave a sudden ringing shout and plunged down the stairs toward the group of gamblers. They opened noisily to receive him.

From a far corner a clash of metal sounded, rhythmic and accompanied by high, ululating shouts. The whole scene swirled with noise, double faces, the ripple of heavy ice-robes, rhythm and melody under a sky shot with dramatic cold light and shadow.

Among these tall, half-serpentine figures, ignored by them, the humans called Khom walked humbly. And Sawyer knew at last the race from which Klai had sprung. The same tilt of cheekbone and the set of the eyes which had so fascinated him looked up now from every face. They were dark people mostly, looking squat among their tall, supercilious gods. They wore dull, dun-colored tunics and long leggings under aprons and smocks. They walked carefully and stood back when the Isier passed.

Beyond this noisy crowd, at the edges of the square, Sawyer had a glimpse of intricately piled buildings, brick and stone, streets diving into rabbit-warren fastnesses and twisting out of sight. Down the dim tunnels and among the roofs, lights were beginning to go on in the darkening air. Far off, above the buildings, lifted a tremendous crown of towers like ice, or glass. They flashed diamond-bright in the fierce, cold light that slanted between the clouds.

"The Temple," Klai murmured at his side. "You see? When the ceremony begins, the Opening of the Well, you can see the reflections of the Firebirds shining up to the very tops of the towers. Half the city's lighted by it."

Around them, on the steps, the emerging and awakening Isier still streamed down toward the square. And just below them, half-hesitating, Nethe stood looking back. Her vivid, dangerous face with its Etruscan smile and its enormous, snake-like eyes was luminous with anger, and perhaps with fear. She was glaring past them, at the curtains from which they had come. Turning, Sawyer saw Alper's heavy face looking through the fluttering folds. He moved back when he met Nethe's glare. Nethe hissed a furious burst of words in

42

her own tongue and then twisted like a serpent, turning to glance down into the square.

Klai's cold hand slipped trembling into Sawyer's.

"Look," she said in a frightened whisper. "The Goddess!" Suddenly she ducked her head and pulled the fur-lined hood of the coat she still wore over her face. "Maybe no one will know me!" she said frantically. "I'll hide if I can. Oh, if only grandfather knew!"

Sawyer pressed her hand in useless consolation and looked down over the square at the double file of tall Isier figures which moved forward at a rapid stride through the crowd. They walked in a V-formation, opening up a way with the apex of their lines. The long robes swirled as they strode.

The apex of the oncoming V reached the foot of the steps. It opened. And the appalling figure of the Isier Goddess stepped forth. . . .

For an instant complete disbelief made Sawyer's mind reel. Disbelief of this whole dreamlike world. The ground did not exist under him, nor the sky overhead. He *must* still be in Fortuna; this incredible place called Khom'ad had no reality at all. In the whole drifting journey down the ice-tunnel he had been sure, under the surface of his mind, that at the far end they would come out into the open, snowy wastes around the Pile. Or into some cavern at best, down under the mine. But this was no cavern. The sky was overhead, and the sun could be seen sinking in it. What sun? The sun that shone on Earth? Where was Khom'ad? Where—

The Goddess spoke, a deep and hollow and resonantly musical sound.

"*Klai,*" she said. And the girl shuddered heavily, sighed and dropped her hood.

The Goddess was a tall, swaying column of total darkness which balanced on its height a blank, pale, passionless face with two great green eyes faceted like emeralds and too bright to look into. At first glance, she seemed not to be there at all except as the pale mask floating upon a column of blindness. The eyes of the beholder dazzled and tried in vain to focus upon the garment that clothed her. The straight-falling robe was black, but a black out of which all light had so entirely gone that it could hardly be perceived at all.

Where the figure stood, a hole in the air seemed to stand too.

The Goddess had no face. Hers was the only figure here to wear two masks, fronting both forward and back. In the oval openings where the eyes should be two large, flat lenses caught the light and shot it forth again blindingly, emerald-green, faceted. Sawyer wondered what the world must look like through those cut surfaces. Did the Goddess see as a spider does, in solid banks of complex, faceted images?

The green gaze like two tangible rays of light touched Klai, knew her, dismissed her for the moment and dwelt speculatively on Sawyer. He felt burned where the green fire touched him. As the gaze moved past him, Nethe burst into sudden, impassioned speech, trying in vain to draw the eyes of the Goddess to herself. It was useless. The gaze moved on toward the curtains out of which the drifting Isier came. . . .

Sawyer turned to watch. Alper's face was dimly visible, peering out, trying with a fatal curiosity to see what was happening. He saw. He met the searching green beams that swept from the sockets of the Goddess-mask, and Sawyer saw him go rigid for an instant, and then move stiffly forward.

Like a man hypnotized—perhaps he *was* hypnotized—he stepped out between the curtains and came down the steps slowly, moving with an automaton's gait. Nethe's breath hissed softly through her teeth. Alper's hand was in his pocket, and the Firebird was nowhere to be seen. . . .

The Goddess spoke for the second time, her voice hollow and resonant inside the mask. The column of her guards moved forward. And with a sudden, sinuous leap, Nethe sprang between the three humans on the step and the advancing Isier. She screamed angry commands at them, her voice running deep with latent music even when she was angriest. The guards hesitated, looked toward the Goddess. It crossed Sawyer's mind that if Nethe were really destined to assume that terrible mask and robe in three days, the guards might well pause before flatly disobeying her.

The Goddess spoke again, dispassionately. Nethe swooped forward toward her, in a swirl of ice-white robes The two stood face to face for a long moment, each swaying just a little, like two hooded cobras poised to strike.

"She's threatening the Goddess," Klai whispered faintly. "She's saying what she'll do after—Oh, wait! Listen!"

The Goddess spoke in a voice that rang across the square. Nethe swayed back, hissing. From the crowd, Isier and Khom alike, a low gasp rose.

"What is it?" Sawyer demanded urgently. "What did she say?"

"Hush," Klai said anxiously. "Let me listen. She—she isn't going to surrender the Double Mask without a fight. She challenges Nethe to the Unsealing of the Well. That means one of them will die. It's her right. If she wants to take the chance, she can do it. She—"

"I thought these Isier were immortal?" Sawyer said.

"To outsiders, yes. But there's one weapon that destroys them. The reigning Goddess controls it. I don't know what it is. No Khom knows. If the Goddess unleashes the weapon she can be destroyed by it herself, of course. But she makes the challenge anyway. She says she'll kill Nethe at the Unsealing of the Well, or die at Nethe's hands." Klai drew another of those deep, unsteady breaths. She laughed, a weak, small sound. "I'll have a grandstand seat for a big event," she said, smiling up at Sawyer.

"What do you mean," he asked, clasping her hand harder. "What's the—the Unsealing?"

"A ceremony," Klai told him. "Where they need sacrifices, naturally! And the Goddess knew me. Now I've got something to look forward to!"

Nethe had gone rigid before the triumphant, challenging figure she confronted. She seemed imperceptibly to shrink into herself a little, to draw back. Klai laughed. Nethe heard, for she turned her head slightly and the little lamps at her ears swung backward against the cheeks of her mask. She hissed once more, a chain of furious, musical phrases at the Goddess. Then she whirled toward the waiting group on the steps. She shot one slanted, lethal glance from her snake-like eyes at Klai. The girl caught her breath and huddled against Sawyer. Nethe's crescent-smile deepened ominously. The large, luminous eyes moved to Alper, still standing rigid, facing the Goddess.

"I'll get to you later," she said in a rapid, low voice.

45

"When you're questioned, *keep quiet about the Firebird*. Remember what I say or we'll all die. Alper, do you hear me?"

Numbly he nodded his heavy head.

She turned away and swept down toward the Goddess as a file of the Isier guards came upward toward the humans. The lofty, inhuman faces did not glance down, but their hands were like cold iron on Sawyer's arms, urging him forward down the steps. Alper came slowly awake and struggled briefly, and Klai collapsed in the grip of the oblivious gods. Half stumbling, half walking, they went rapidly down into the square in the strong, cold hands of the Isier.

The sunset grew lurid behind the storm-clouds as the Goddess's men took their captives down winding streets toward the glass towers of the temple. It was darkening fast here, and lights went on one by one as the long file wound its way among the evening crowds. Here in the narrow byways the prisoners were led single file, so that Sawyer and Klai could no longer speak. The girl had thrown her hood back now, and was scanning the familiar streets anxiously, hoping hard for recognition.

Sawyer walked in a dream, hearing unfamiliar speech all around him, seeing strange lights go on behind curtain and colored shade in the mysteries of these unknown houses. It seemed a very real and solid world.

Music in extraordinary rhythms, at extraordinary pitches, played on instruments Sawyer could not even guess at, sounded behind windows glowing deep crimson or bright green with lamplight. The smells of unfamiliar cooking drifted through the streets, mingled with the poignantly familiar fragrance of woodsmoke. Small boys with shrill voices vended something out of wire-net cones which Sawyer could not see clearly. They dodged to and fro in the crowds, doing a brisk evening business.

But mostly the crowd fell silent and melted miraculously off the streets as the Isiers passed with their captives. Sawyer met many grave, quiet gazes along the way, sympathy offered helplessly by the humble folk who could no more than pity the captives and hope fervently to be spared themselves. Once, from a high window, someone threw a spotted purple fruit that thumped against the black-facing mask of the Isier just before Sawyer. The man turned quickly, marked the window with a serene eye, and went on. Sawyer felt a cold chill down his back.

Just as they reached the entry to the street where the Temple stood, a solemn roll of thunder shook the city and a slanting shower of rain swept across the rooftops, colored crimson by the sunset. Windows slammed against it, doors banged, women called anxiously and children answered. It was an emptied street that the captives left as they reached the Temple gates, with a shower of blood-red rain falling over it.

The gates were like glass, or ice, and soared to a mighty arch almost gothic in its intricacy of mounting and interlacing tracery, all colorless in itself but glowing ominously now with the red light of evening. A curtain of copper mesh hung in tremendous folds inside the whole gate, closing it from the street.

The party halted. The foremost Isier pursed his thin, curved lips and whistled like a flute, with a woodwind tremolo, very clean and sweet. Afterward they stood waiting in the rain.

Just as the copper curtain began to quiver and part, a disturbance began at the mouth of an alley at Sawyer's elbow. He could not see very clearly into it because of the slanting light and the rain, but there was a sudden rabble of men and animals rushing toward them, in a tumult of shouting and whinnying. Cartwheels rumbled noisily between the reverberating walls, and all the noises multiplied with echoes.

As nearly as Sawyer could tell, several carts loaded high with something that looked and smelled very like wet raw wool were hurtling toward them behind wildly running horses, little shaggy beasts incongruously spotted like leopards. In the foremost cart rode a plump elderly man in the apron-like tunic of a street vendor. His feet were braced on the cart's edge, and he bent forward to lash the leopard-spotted ponies to even greater speed, his thin fringe of white whiskers streaming in the wind.

Behind him rumbled other carts, men shouting and running at top speed to keep pace. And behind them men shouted and dogs barked, while windows flew open to let interested heads pop out. There was complete bedlam quite suddenly, between the Isier's whistle and the first quiver of the gate curtain.

Then the whole noisy rabble was upon them. The excited little horses plunged kicking and snorting through the column waiting before the Temple. Every dog within earshot had already begun to yap earsplittingly, the horses whinnied with a sound almost like a human scream, and the shouting men burst out among the careening carts, raining blows upon the horses, kicking at the dogs which had sprung up so magically underfoot.

Even the lordly Isiers gave way before this onslaught. Sawyer felt his elbow gripped in an iron clasp and let himself be pulled sidewise against the wall of the nearest house. The Isiers were shouting too now, in deep, bell-like roars of anger and command. A horse kicked frantically. Its cart overturned with a tremendous clatter, and great wool-bales rolled heavily in the wet street.

By sheer chance, in all this tumult, Sawyer caught Klai's eye. Her face was electrified with excitement and dawning hope. She leaned forward as far as she could in the grip of her captor, scanning the faces of the running men. Sawyer saw the first glow of hope beginning to dim. He thought incongruously of the unhappy Lise Bolkonskaya with her inadequate upper lip and her *seduisant* charms, and then lurched heavily against the grip of the Isier behind him.

The lurch became a genuine skid as his foot struck a puddle of crimson rain on the pavement. The Isier staggered, trying to hold him up. Sawyer jerked the Isier a little forward in an apparent attempt to regain balance, caught the tall creature across his hip as they fell together, and slid with him full-tilt into the Isier who held Klai.

It was the chance she had been waiting for. With a tremendous wriggle, like a rabbit deftly skinning itself in a single motion, she writhed out of her fur-lined coat, and with an agile bound was at the side of the foremost cart as it thundered past. The plump old man shouted "Klai!" and bent to sweep her up. With a leap and a wriggle over the sideboard she made her goal, and the cart thundered on

48

triumphantly, never slackening speed. *Grandpa*, Sawyer thought, as the crowd of drivers, shouting with a note of triumph now, closed in after her.

All hope of following them failed as a hand like iron closed on Sawyer's shoulder. He gave a mental shrug and scrambled to his feet. The tumult swept away up another alley and died as if by magic. Two of the Isier looped up their ropes and set off at a long, silent pace after the vanished uproar. A few of the more hysterical dogs followed down the alley, shrilling, but most of them were quiet now, and the whole episode might well have been a dream.

Except for one thing, Sawyer thought. Klai's empty coat, its furry hood drooping forward over its collapsed chest with a pathetic look of dejection, still dangling from the hands of the surprised Isier who had held her. Sawyer was aware of a sharp stab of nostalgia, seeing that familiar garment tenantless, the girl as gone as if she had never existed, swallowed up in a city that was both hers and utterly strange to her.

It had all happened so quickly that the curtain was still parting slowly in the center and drawing back while the uproar faded into stillness. Inside the flickering mesh a glassy corridor stretched. Sawyer's captor pushed him forward under the faintly crackling copper folds. He glanced back at Klai's abandoned coat, lying face down in the street in an attitude of despair. Then the curtains swept shut again and all sound from the outer world ended abruptly.

Alper sat on a low ledge of glass in a bare glass cell and stared at Sawyer. Sawyer sat on the floor in the opposite corner, hugged his knees and stared at Alper.

Alper said, "You're a fool."

Sawyer paid no attention.

"You helped her escape," Alper pursued. "That was idiotic of you. We'll probably both suffer for it."

Sawyer let his gaze rove once more around the bare, smooth walls, translucent and faintly green, only to return to Alper's face without encountering anything worth lingering on in the journey. There was probably a door in the wall. They had entered by a door. But it had sealed itself shut so thoroughly as to be quite invisible now. Light came through an unseen source, high up near one corner of the cell.

"I don't like this either," he said slowly. "Not one bit. I want out just as much as you do. It looks to me as though we're both in the same boat now."

"Boat!" Alper said. "World! This isn't Earth. I don't understand any—"

"You probably understand more about it than I do. If we intend to try to make any plans, you'd better tell me what you know. About Nethe, for example. Didn't she give you any hint that this—this world existed?"

"No," Alper said sullenly. "She came to me at Fortuna, just as you saw her. Shadowy. I thought I was dreaming at first. But when she touched me with her closed fist and I felt energy beginning to pour through me—" He glanced in triumph at the Firebird in his hand—"after that, I gave her anything she wanted."

"Uranium ore?"

"Yes. She didn't want uranium mined out and taken away, and that's why I was trying to close the mine, of course. But I had no idea of—all this."

"We'd better start getting used to it," Sawyer said. "And we'll have a better chance working together than as enemies. So how about a truce? Obviously I can't send a report back to Toronto now. We may be here for quite a while."

Alper nodded grudgingly.

"Fine," Sawyer said. "Then the first thing is to take this transceiver off my head."

"No," Alper said.

"Why not? Controlling me won't help you a bit right now, will it?"

"It might stop you from trying to kill me," Alper said, his grey eyes wary with suspicion. "I know what I'd do in your shoes, young man."

"You're a fool," Sawyer observed.

Alper thought for a time.

"All right," he said. "A truce might be the best thing right now. Say we do work together, from now on. But the transceiver stays on your head—as insurance. Now. You spoke about making plans. What, for example?"

50

Sawyer wrapped his arms around his knees again.

"The only practical one I can suggest, at present," he said sourly, "is waiting."

VI

THEY HAD BEEN SITTING silent for about ten minutes, exchanging occasional looks of dislike, when a curious humming sound began to be heard from a corner of the cell opposite to the door by which they had entered. Both turned to look. Low down in the corner a square of the wall about three feet across had begun to shimmer violently. As they watched, the surface of the square became translucent, showed for a moment or two a complex hexagonal crystalline pattern, and then broke up entirely into a pale green vapor which puffed outward into the cell with a burst of quick heat that brought sweat to their foreheads.

The heat dissipated rapidly. The air was hazy with green vapor, and the square in the wall stood open and empty. Like the dry-ice of solid carbon dioxide, the molecules of the substance making up the wall had apparently been moved to evaporate abruptly without the need of melting into liquid form. The wall had altered in form but not in substance, and the vapor which had in its solid condition been impermeable now hung like a green fog in the air, leaving an exit open.

A supercilious, glass-crowned Isier head now appeared through the opening and regarded them with complete objectivity, as a human might glance into a chicken-coop and observe the inmates. Even that god-like brow, however, was sweating beneath the crown. The heat which had vaporized the wall must have been considerable.

The large, half-lidded eyes of the Isier considered Sawyer coldly, moved to Alper, summed him up in a glance and apparently decided that he was the man the Isier had come to find, for without entering the cell any farther, the demigod brought a long non-human hand into sight and tossed into Alper's lap a package about ten inches square. It was black, and it shimmered dazzlingly.

51

Before anyone could move or speak the Isier head withdrew, supercilious to the last. For an instant the opening in the wall stood empty. Then a gust of intense cold soughed through it into the cell. All the molecules of the green vapor, which had been rioting energetically in the heat, now obeyed the laws of their kind by condensing with a rapidity unknown upon Earth. In the blink of an eye the vapor had been sucked backward into the emptiness whence it had come, the air was clear again and the wall unbroken.

Alper touched the package on his knee gingerly. He gave Sawyer a suspicious glance. The package solved his problem at this point by collapsing suddenly from its solidly compact cube into a limp, unfolding bundle of shimmering black cloth, so totally black that the eye could not fix upon it, but slid repeatedly away for lack of anything to focus on. The bundle had been wrapped, apparently, not in a confining paper or carton, but in a little cubical force-field of its own. When this unique wrapping let go, something like a cloak of remarkable volume for the original size of the bundle spilled over Alper's knees and onto the floor. Out of its unfolding center a little cone of white paper popped with a brisk snap, and unfolded itself noisily, lying flat.

Alper took it up by its extreme corners. There was writing on the white surface. Alper's eyes moved rapidly down the lines. Then a look of triumph lighted his face. He laughed in a sudden bark of elation and glanced up at Sawyer, his hand moving in the same instant to his pocket.

Thunder and lightning. Down between the lobes of his brain Sawyer felt jagged sheets of blindness flashing. His own blood-beat, amplified to a volume of noise like the crash of doom, blanked out everything before him.

But this time, he was ready for it. Almost ready—as ready as any man could be for the crack of Thor's hammer on his bare brain. He saw Alper's hand move. He read aright the expression on Alper's face in the instant before the motion started. And the decision which had been crystallizing in his mind ever since the last time Alper had used the transceiver took over his muscles and his nerves without any need for further thought.

Before the thunder split his skull apart he was off the

floor; he was in mid-air when the lightning struck. And Alper's attention was partially distracted by the message in his hand and the mystifying cascade of blackness across his knees. If it was a half-unconscious man who struck him in that long leap across the cell, it was still a heavy and a desperate man.

The impact knocked Alper sidewise. He flung up both startled hands to fend Sawyer off, and with the release of contact in his pocket, the thunder ceased abruptly in Sawyer's head.

It was no fault of Sawyer's that he did not kill the man. He meant to. As Alper struggled up to meet the attack Sawyer knocked him sidewise with an edge-of-the-hand blow meant for the side of Alper's neck. Luckily for Alper it struck him across the cheek-bone instead as he rose. Sawyer's other hand sank into his belly, doubling him forward, and Sawyer's lifted knee smashed him squarely in the face.

Sawyer bent over the writhing body on the floor, hand lifted for the sidewise crack across the base of the brain that would certainly finish him. And then caution returned in a faint glimmer of warning. If Alper died, would the transceiver explode in his own head?

Carefully, he clipped Alper on the jaw. And once again. He paused, watching, making sure that Alper was unconscious. Then with rough hands he turned the man over and reached into that fatal coat pocket from which the thunder in his brain had been triggered. He found a small flat case the size of a wristwatch. Very cautiously he put a feather-weight of pressure on it. An ominous humming sounded in his head as his own blood and breath roared loud in the cavities of his skull.

He leaned forward, releasing his finger's pressure. His ear was close to the coat pocket.

"Alper," he said softly. "Alper?"

From the little case, a thin voice that was his own echoed the name. So it was a radio receiver, too. Alper had not lied about that. The multi-purpose transceiver on his own head was also a microphone that could betray him to Alper no matter how far away he might go.

He drew a deep breath and pulled the case out of Alper's

pocket. It came easily. It was not attached by any visible or tangible cord. But as it left the damping influence of Alper's body-field the low humming began again, and the farther it was removed the louder the humming grew. Sawyer stepped back two paces and the humming became low thunder. He shook his head violently and stepped back another pace.

Then he leaped blindly for Alper's body and thrust the case back into the pocket it had come from. The violence in his head ceased as softly as if it had never been.

So he was in a complete dilemma. He could not endure the coercion of the transceiver any longer, and he could not endure the only means of stopping it. He flexed his hand eagerly and looked down at the helpless form of his tormenter, whom he dared not kill, for fear of splitting his own brain apart.

Alper had said there was a shut-off switch in the control case. He had added that Houdini couldn't locate it and only a differential analyzer could find the combination. Sawyer gingerly reached into Alper's pocket again and drew out the flat metal case.

Perhaps the secret of the shut-off switch's camouflage was in its simplicity. Or perhaps that was the one point on which Alper *had* lied, Sawyer thought—perhaps there was no shut-off switch. He studied the case carefully. Even with all the time in the world, he wondered if he would be able to locate the switch and find the combination—if it existed.

Ten minutes later, convinced of failure, he put the case back in Alper's pocket and turned to the note that had touched off Alper's attack on him.

It rustled crisply between his fingers. It was smooth and white, and the writing upon it was ordinary English in a curiously looping hand, traced as if by fingers that had not learned English script until lately. It was, however, perfectly coherent.

"Alper: I will save you if I can. I need your help. I want the Firebird you stole. You want to live. We can make a fair trade if you do exactly as I tell you. Here is a black cloak such as the Temple's servants wear on private errands for the Goddess. Within limits it should make you moderately invisible after dark. You can open the wall by pressing one of the studs along the hem of the cloak against any spot that glows when the stud approaches it. Let go of the stud as soon as it adheres or you will burn your fingers. When the hood covers your head you will hear a humming signal that will guide you to me if you keep it constant as you walk. Stay in the shadows, speak to no one and answer no questions. You don't need to, for you will be wearing the Goddess's robe."

The last paragraph was underlined heavily. "I can do nothing for you unless this is kept secret. Make sure that the man with you is dead before you go. The Firebird will give you enough energy to kill him. But open the Firebird only when you and the other Earthman are alone, or it will be taken from you by the Isier guards; and do not leave it open longer than is necessary to gain the energy you need."

The signature at the end of this businesslike message was simply, "*Nethe.*"

Sawyer looked down at Alper and with a strong effort controlled the new impulse to kill him. He stopped and shook out the cloak. The thing was light and fine and of a smoothness and blackness so complete that even held this close he could not persuade his gaze to focus clearly on it.

He had no idea what lay outside or what Nethe's real plans were, but anything seemed preferable to helplessness and captivity here. The only drawback was that no matter where he went or how successful he might be in winning his way to comparative freedom, he would have won nothing worth having if Alper could split his skull wide open whenever the whim seized him.

Sawyer shook his head again, hard, quite sure that there was an answer in it if he could only shake the right idea into place. And perhaps the shake did it. For in another moment he suddenly laughed, dropped the cloak, and stooped to roll Alper over, freeing his pockets. He found the golden Firebird device in the third pocket he tried.

With Alper's own pen he wrote a note on the back of Nethe's paper:

"Thanks for the cloak and the Firebird. I wish I could have killed you. I know my life depends on yours. I'm now putting you in a position where yours depends on mine—it's safer for me than depending on any truces you make. Use the transceiver on me once more and you'll never know what became of the Firebird. Let me alone and if my plan succeeds I'll come back for you. This is the only bargain I can offer. Take it or leave it. But I warn you. If you touch the transceiver's control again, you'll never touch the Firebird. You have enough energy from it now to last you until we meet again. Whether you get any more depends on me. Remember that before you use the transceiver."

There was no need to sign the note. Sawyer wrapped it around the control case in Alper's pocket. Then he shook out the cloak, tossed it about his shoulders, pulled the hood over his head and ran the hem of the cloth through his fingers until he found a row of small, detachable studs.

The wall through which the Isier had come and gone glowed in one spot when the stud approached it. Sawyer touched stud to glow, felt it cling, and jumped back as fast as he could. The wall shimmered with crystalline patterns, the heat burst from it, the pale green vapor formed again and the air-pressure in the cell heightened as the wall grew volatile and the low gateway opened.

Through the haze of solid substance made gaseous enough to pass, Sawyer crawled rapidly. The Firebird in his pocket made a spot of faint, tingling warmth at his side. He had a moment's regret that he had not opened the little, golden miracle to allow the flood of rejuvenating energy to pour through him—Nethe's message had implied that the Firebird gave out no energy unless it was opened. He felt tired and hungry and thirsty, but these matters were not important, compared to the real problem He had a job to do, and he did not quite know how to go about it.

Ahead glimmered light, and the drifting haze of rain.

Rain in long, slanting sheets fell sparkling along the streets in the light from curtained windows. It drummed on the hood Sawyer had drawn over his head, ran in cold streams from his shoulders. sometimes half drowned out the steady buzz that hummed in his ears to summon him to Nethe. He went slowly through the nearly deserted streets, keeping himself oriented by the humming noise that sounded from two small studs sewn into the hood in the vicinity of his ears.

He kept to byways when he could. He had suspended disbelief, because he had to. Obviously he was walking the streets of a city upon a world that could not be his own. The very existence of the Isier proved that. How very unlike his own planet it was he had not yet learned, but he knew enough to go warily.

The Isier seemed to have some command over a technological system. At least, they recognized the conductivity of copper, as in the Temple curtain, for a force which had behaved like electricity. And the vaporization of the cell wall was another trick behind which you would expect a whole recognizable technology to lie. The pressure of stud to wall had clearly excited very rapid molecular activity to the end result of producing heat enough for vaporization. How the reverse action was triggered remained obscure, but condensation certainly stopped the molecules dead in their tracks and restored the former state of matter in the wall.

Still, you couldn't prove anything by the fact that they understood certain chemical and physical properties of matter. Societies may have some touching points in common and yet be totally unintelligible to each other on many levels. Perhaps in each, at sunset, fires would be lighted, meals cooked, lamps would burn, dogs would bark and women would call children in out of a sudden shower. But you could not, by these things alone, guess what values moved the people of an unfamiliar world.

Anyhow, Sawyer thought, somewhere among these wet rooftops was an old man's house where Klai was at this moment probably sitting beside a fire, retelling her dreamlike experiences in a dream-world called Earth.

The humming in his ears hesitated suddenly and then seemed to shift direction. Sawyer turned his head from side to side, puzzled, in an attempt to orient himself by the sound. After a moment he turned at right angles to his original course. Nethe was on the move too, it seemed.

Where was he really going? Violently he wished for the ability to speak the local language. If he could get to Klai and Grandpa, half his problem would be solved. But he could wander forever before sheer chance took him where he wanted to go, and in the meantime Nethe or one of the other Isier would be certain to seize him.

If he didn't turn up at Nethe's rendezvous within a reasonable time, she would probably come to find out why. It seemed at least possible that she could trace him through this cloak as readily as he could trace her. And if he discarded it his only disguise was gone.

But he had something of immense potential value to Nethe —the Firebird. It seemed to Sawyer that the best bet might be to find a hiding place for the Firebird and then meet Nethe, keeping a safe distance from her—he had great respect for the strength in that tornado-like body—and bargain for whatever seemed most desirable. Information, for example, about how the Firebird could be made to open the Gateway back to Earth.

You couldn't plan too far ahead under circumstances like these. There was too much that was totally unknown. It was always possible that Nethe might lean out of the next window he passed, knock him over the head and loot his unconscious body. All he could do was go warily, watch the shadows, and trust that providence would defend the right. Providence in this world seemed to be most unfairly on the side of wrong, though that was a matter of viewpoint.

The key was the Firebird. He didn't dare keep it on him or hide it.

If only Nethe would stay still, he thought irritably, pausing again as the humming veered erratically in his hood. He waited in the wet, deserted street, under a lighted window behind which a baby was crying drearily, until Nethe seemed to halt again and send out the summons more steadily. From beyond a door a dog burst into hysterical yaps as Sawyer passed and scratched in a fury against the lower panels.

As it happened, the same shrill dog gave him his first clue that he was perhaps being followed. The dog subsided after he had passed, only to burst into sudden fresh hysteria when Sawyer was a hundred feet away. He stepped into the deepest shadow he could find and looked back suspiciously. But the shadows gave shelter to his follower too, if he had one, and he saw only the empty street, heard only the furious, muffled yappings and the assault of scratching nails upon a door.

He went on after awhile, because there seemed no alternative. At least, he himself was totally invisible as long as he stayed in the shadows. He kept a careful watch behind him after that.

The faceted thing that linked him to Alper was grotesquely like a third ear laid flat against his very thoughts. What ever he said to Nethe, when he met her, he would be saying to Alper too if Alper chose to listen. And whatever Nethe said, Alper would hear. They could make no bargain in which Alper was not a partner. Always supposing, of course, that Alper let him live, once he awoke and found Sawyer and the Firebird gone. But that was an occupational risk Sawyer could not avoid. He could only ignore it, and wait.

Nethe's summons came steadily for about fifteen minutes from the same direction, and Sawyer walked fast, keeping an alert watch, hoping this time to come within earshot of her before she shot off on another erratic flight.

Journey's end came very suddenly.

The signal hummed strong and clear. Sawyer turned a corner and stopped so suddenly his feet skidded on the wet street. He drew back into a doorway and peered out, cursing Nethe silently. For before him a broad, lighted thoroughfare led up to and ended abruptly at a great fortified gate. High stone walls stretched left and right from it. This was clearly the very edge of the city, and for the first time Sawyer realized it was a city that expected trouble from outside.

The gate was high, and closed with enormous iron doors. On the wall-top Khom guards leaned, keeping an intent watch outward, toward some invisible source of danger in the night. Other guards, Khom in metal-studded tunics and carrying what were probably weapons but looked more like tubas, patrolled the gate.

One of the Isier, looming like a god above the short humans, was exchanging words loftily with a Khom officer. There was a great deal of orderly activity, and Sawyer's un-

59

easiness increased. For the summons in his ears seemed to come from directly beyond the gate, from out there in the dark.

Were the Isier searching for Nethe too? What would happen if Sawyer stepped boldly out and handed the Firebird over to this supercilious godling? What, on the other hand, would happen to him if he went blindly in answer to Nethe's summons? He struggled with ambivalent confusion for a while. But if he surrendered now, he would be at the mercy of the unknown. Nethe's reactions at least he could predict to some slight degree. Cautiously he withdrew down the alley. What he wanted now was an unguarded stretch of this wall.

He found it at the end of a quiet alley, got over the wall by way of a handy shed roof, and came down lightly upon wet grass in darkness on the other side. He seemed to be standing in open country, for he could make out rolling treetops, lashed by rain, and a very faint line where sky and land met between two clumps of trees.

A pinpoint of light flashed and went out again near the trees.

"Here I am," Nethe's voice said impatiently. "Come on. Hurry! Straight toward me and you're all right."

Cautiously, taking his time, Sawyer set out toward the light. Wet grass was slippery underfoot. The robe he wore was waterproof, but trickles of rain beat in his face under the edges of the hood and wind whipped its folds around his wet legs. He could make out only a dim, pale blur of a face under the trees. Between the tossing branches a brighter luminescence glowed faintly, as if a large body of water stretched away from a nearby shore, gathering all the light in the sky to its reflecting surface.

When he was about twenty feet awy, Nethe said, "Wait," and was silent for a moment while he stood there with the wind whipping the cloak around his legs and the rain streaming in his face.

Then Nethe laughed, a soft, low, triumphant sound.

"All right," she said. "Run!"

Something about that laugh, and the tone she spoke in, rang a warning bell far back in Sawyer's mind. He moved forward obediently, but he did not run. He felt a strange sort of tingling caution all over his body, as if the nerve-endings in his skin were desperately alert to catch the first hint of a danger he suspected but could not identify. For some senseless reason he found himself counting his strides as he moved rapidly forward toward the trees.

Seven long steps thudded softly on grass and solid ground. The eighth came down on empty space and he pitched forward into nothingness. Above him the low laugh sounded again, gloating with triumph, and footsteps drummed rapidly on turf as Nethe hurried forward to watch him fall.

VII

WITH DESPERATE, RAPID CLARITY, like a man drowning, Sawyer took in at one whirling glance what lay below him. In one burst of understanding he saw almost every detail of what lay below.

The luminous void beyond the trees was not an ocean. It was an empty abyss of air. The trees rimmed what must be the farthest outpost of solid land on this outer shell of creation where the city stood. But below, infinitely far below, in infinitely wide space, swam another planet. Clouds floated milkily in a pale silver sky. Some of them must be storm-clouds, for they were ominously black, and drifting close below him.

He had fallen through some break in the soil a little way inland from the crumbling edges of the world. Nethe must have lined herself carefully up with that well-opening to infinity, deliberately urged him to run so that he would be certain to pitch free, with no chance to catch himself.

And for an endless, curdling moment of sheer panic he did fall free. Then something whipped by his face and with the drowning man's instant reflex he clenched both hands into the netted mass that had lashed against him as he dropped.

The fall broke. With a neck-wrenching jerk, momentum snapped him around in a wide pendulum-swing. Far below, the distant world seemed to lurch up toward its northern

61

horizon, climbing half the sky, only to fall back again sickeningly in the opposite direction. Sawyer shut his eyes and clawed both hands deep into the saving nets that still snapped and crackled terrifyingly, letting him down with little sudden jerks as more of their filaments gave beneath his weight. With infinite caution he opened his eyes. So precarious was his support that the very act of lifting his lids might, he felt, put a fatal added weight upon the thing which held him.

Now he could see. A dim, luminous glow filled the whole vast, incredible emptiness over which he dangled. Straight down under his swinging feet the distant world floated. This net he hung on seemed to be an interlaced mesh of tree roots. The shell of soil must be very thin here, so near the edge. The trees grew partly in soil and partly in air, their roots dangling in the void. There hung a little distance away, just within reach, if he dared reach, thicker and still stronger strands. But at the moment it seemed to him that it would be absolutely fatal to move a muscle.

A little shower of pebbles rattled down on his head and shoulders. Greatly daring, he tilted his head back a little. Over the crumbling edge of this air-well down which he had fallen, Nethe's bright, dangerous face peered hopefully. He saw disappointment cloud it. He still lived.

She said, "Oh," in a rather dashed voice. Sawyer said nothing. He dared not speak. He was measuring the distance to the stronger roots, and wondering what would happen if he supported his whole weight on the meshes he held with one hand while he stretched for the security of the larger ones. He thought he would fall.

Nethe said, "Alper?" in an uncertain voice. Sawyer did not answer. She said again, "Alper? Is it you?"

Sawyer felt the soft burning of the Firebird against his side, and his frozen mind began slowly to make plans again. It seemed ridiculous to suppose that he had any future to plan for, but the human mind is a resilient creation.

Nethe said, amid a shower of pebbles as she leaned farther out, "It isn't Alper. You made a mistake, didn't you? Sprang another man's trap." She laughed. "Shall I help you up?"

He said nothing even then. He knew she would not, probably could not, help him. If anything saved him, it must be himself. Already his arm-muscles were complaining and he knew he could hold on only a little longer. He began very, very cautiously to swing himself on the crackling roots, starting a new pendulum motion that with luck might carry him within reach of the strong taproot dangling an arms-length away.

"If you brought the Firebird," Nethe said persuasively from above, "I'll help you up. Have you got it? Oh, you must have it. You're no fool. Hand it up and I'll pull you back to solid ground again."

He did not glance up. Now he was swinging quite perceptibly, and the roots were holding. Most of them, anyhow. He gave himself one last reckless swing and with the strength of despair launched himself through emptiness straight toward those heavy strands that could save him, for a moment or two, if he caught both hands about them just right.

The void swam dizzily below him. The roots flew past his face. Then with a satisfying, noisy smack his two groping palms struck together around the thick taproot and he hung swaying and shivering, his eyes shut and his cheek pressed hard against the fringed and hairy surface of the root.

A gasp sounded above. More pebbles showered. Then several clods fell spinning into the luminous abyss and Nethe was heard to swear musically in her own tongue and to scramble as if for support. Sawyer laughed. He felt much better now. He had little reason for confidence, but at least he could depend on the strength of his support.

"Are you all right?" Nethe called from above. "I tell you, if you'll hand up the Firebird I'll save you. Don't you want to be saved? I meant to get rid of Alper, not you."

She talked on, her voice showing a hint of panic, but Sawyer had a new task to hand and he closed his ears temporarily to her. He had caught the dangling root between clenched knees and ankles, like a rope, freeing one hand. Now he was scanning the overhang of the soil a little way from his face, out of which the roots dangled. A round, smooth hole, like a burrow, had attracted his notice and a dim, vengeful idea was taking shape in his mind. He put out his free hand and thrust an exploring finger into the burrow.

There was a scrabbling inside. He took his finger out,

and a small, beady-eyed head followed curiously. Two tiny, hand-like paws clutched the mouth of the burrow and a small, toothy creature like a squirrel, its fur fluffy and barred like an owl's feathers, peered out at him with an overpowering interest. Clearly this was an entirely new experience in the life of barred squirrels. It turned its head alertly to one side and then the other, observing the dangling man with great intentness.

Sawyer chirruped to it. This threw the squirrel into an unexpected panic. It whirled in the narrow space of the burrow, flashed a large, feathery tail in his face and prepared to scramble for its life. It misgauged. The frantic hind feet skidded on emptiness and for a moment both squirrel and man hung supended in empty air.

Sawyer put up a hand and pushed the little creature gently back into its burrow. The tiny, cold feet kicked desperately against his palm for a moment. Then it got purchase and vanished up its burrow in a shower of crumbling earth.

Sawyer craned to squint after it.

There was a rock of about the right size half-embedded in the overhang a foot away. He worked it loose and fitted it into the burrow, pushing it up as far as it would go. Then he reached into his pocket, moving with great caution, and pulled out the golden bar which was the Firebird.

It was warm against his fingers. It glinted faintly in the grey light of the abyss.

He pressed it gently and felt the bars move apart in his fingers. For an instant the dazzling wings sprang open between thumb and forefinger, very near his face. A light like sunshine bathed him, showing up every glittering grain of soil in the overhang so near his head. And a wonderful fount of sheer strength poured through him gloriously. . . .

"The Firebird!" Nethe cried, above him and out of sight. She must be able to see the radiance though she could not see the device itself. There was a soft thud as she threw herself flat on the lip of the shaft. "You have it!" she cried. "I see the fire! Give it to me and I'll save you!"

But Sawyer even in his extremity knew better than that. He dared not let the Firebird stay open more than the few

64

seconds necessary to replenish his failing strength. He did not know what dangers lay latent in it. He had a horrid vision of the winged Firebirds swarming about him out of nowhere, out of some Gateway opened in infinity, while he hung helpless to fight them off.

He snapped the bright wings shut. The fountain of energy died, but that pouring of sheer power seemed to have stored itself in his nerves and muscles, for he felt marvelously refreshed, no longer hungry or thirsty.

At any rate, he thought, Nethe was not going to get the Firebird.

He had been looking for a safe hiding place. Now that it was too late, he had found the ideal spot. He pushed the closed golden bar of the talisman into the burrow, digging it firmly into the soil against the rock. Then he found a second rock and jammed it tightly in after the first.

After that, he tried to climb the rope-like root, but the extra energy he had gained brought him only up to the edge of the overhang which began to crumble precariously as he dangled, the root slipping and jolting. He stopped climbing and simply hung on till the dirt stopped showering past him. Above him, there was more of an opening now, and he thought he caught a glimpse of Nethe.

Pretty problem.

Certainly he couldn't hold on forever here. But if he fell, she wouldn't get the Firebird. Its hiding place might be precarious. It too might fall. The squirrel might tunnel around the rock, guided by its insatiable curiosity, and become the wealthiest squirrel in creation by finding the Firebird for itself. In any case Nethe would not get it.

So, he thought grimly, he was in a position to bargain. He turned gingerly on his root and craned up the air-well.

"Nethe," he called. "Can you hear me?"

Her brilliant face appeared like magic over the grassy verge. The grass dripped, and showers of rain drove now and then down the open well and blew in gusts past Sawyer's cheek.

"If you can get me up," he told Nethe, "I'll bargain with you."

She stretched out a demanding hand.

"I don't trust you. Give me the Firebird first."

Sawyer sighed. "All right. You'll have to stretch a little farther, though. Here, reach!"

The smooth, narrow, subtly distorted hand waved blindly a foot above his face. Sawyer laughed aloud and seized her around the wrist with a desperate grip. He pulled, one threatening, experimental tug.

"Got you now!" he said. "Pull me up or we both go down."

The scream of sheer fury that rang out from her just above his head made him jump convulsively. In the same instant the arm he held lashed into frenzies of writhing in a wild effort to shake him off. It was like holding a twisting serpent. The root he hung upon swayed and jolted, began ominously to creak. His own teeth were rattling with the violence of the struggle. He hung on for dear life, shouting above the furious, hissing curses she was gasping out as she fought:

"Stop it! Nethe, stop it! Hold still or we're both done for! Pull me up!"

"I can't pull you up, you fool," Nethe said wildly.

"That's interesting, in view of the bargain you were trying to make." Sawyer told her, locking his grip harder around the lashing wrist. "Now—I come up or you come down."

He heard the breath hiss through her teeth. He smiled up into the brilliant face straining down above him, almost too bright to look at because of the blaze in her large, inhuman eyes and the look of incandescence behind the fierce grimace. Looking at her, his heart sank a little. He thought. "No one with a face like that could ever give in. She won't. She'd rather die."

"I'm slipping," he told her in an almost conversational voice. "This root's slippery and my hand's sweating. Last chance, Nethe."

The baleful eyes flashed at him, flashed past him into the abyss. The root was slipping through his fingers faster and faster. Nethe slid farther over the edge, hissing furiously. She was half-way over the verge now, and the luminous earrings swung forward like tiny lamps to light their way to destruction. Then Sawyer felt the root quiver between his fingers, heard it snap.

"Well, it was an interesting life, while it lasted," he said mildly, looking up into Nethe's face.

Then the root broke, and for a dizzying second they swung suspended, held only by Nethe's furious grip on some other anchoring root invisible to Sawyer. A look he could not read crossed her face fleetingly. He saw that she gave one downward glance into the abyss. He saw the look of brief, half-incredulous, exultant triumph light her blazing face.

Nethe laughed—and let go.

Which of the things that flashed through his mind came first in importance as he fell? He could not be sure. Time too seemed to have broken free of chronology and stood still around him.

He saw in the opening of the air-well, as Nethe's body whipped through, a man's dark face with a pointed cap above it, peering over the edge of the dripping grass, watching them go down. He saw it with photographic clarity, noting how every detail stood out even as the face and the ragged hole it peered through receded and dwindled above him into something as tiny as the world at the wrong end of a telescope. The watcher's chin rested on the dark, wet grass as he lay flat, looking over the edge of the world, and the grass was like a dripping beard under his chin. Beard and all, he shot away upward to a pinpoint and then whirled clockwise across the sky and vanished.

All around them as they dropped turning through the abyss Nethe's long, ringing scream of laughter echoed. They trailed it like a comet's tail of clear sound.

As they shot downward through the whistling air, that dark storm-cloud which Sawyer had been dimly aware of under him all this while seemed to be floating to intercept them squarely. It shot upward to receive them. Was this why Nethe had laughed and let go, after her incredulous, triumphant glance downward? Even if it was, what use would a cloud be to save them?

It was, Sawyer realized with unwondering surprise, a tree-bearing cloud. . . .

Quite suddenly branches were crackling all around him. Leaves whipped past his face. A deep cradle of limbs bowed strongly beneath the impact of his fall, received him, and

67

sprang upward, tossing him into the air again. He thought, "When the bough breaks, the cradle will fall." But the trees of this world were friendly to him if the people were not. Twice they intercepted his fall. What good a cloud-borne tree would do him, ultimately seemed doubtful. But it was comforting to feel branches under him.

"Good trees," he thought approvingly. "Kind, clever, intelligent trees, hold me up."

The tree at this point cracked him sharply across the head with a broken limb.

For once in his life Sawyer was very grateful indeed for the oblivion that swallowed him up.

He seemed to be lying on a hard, uneven pavement. Shadows flickered across it in a silvery gray dimness. Paved clouds were wholly outside his experience and he tried to lift his head to see more, whereupon a hand slammed his skull down ringingly upon the stones.

"Where is it?" Nethe's voice demanded in a hot, fierce hiss. She must have been ransacking his coat, for she let go so suddenly that he rolled over hard upon uneven rocks, and stars swam before his dazed eyes. "What did you do with the Firebird? I know you had it. Where is it now?"

She bent over him, her blazing gaze a foot above his, the bright lanterns at her ears sending patterns of light into his eyes. Above her in a silvery twilight dark trees tossed. Through them, lowering like a storm-cloud to end all storm-clouds, he could see the black hanging bulk of the upper world, perhaps fifty feet overhead. Rain shot down past its verge in misty gusts.

"Maybe I dropped it," Sawyer said, struggling up. "Where are we? On a cloud?"

"We're on one of the floating islands," Nethe told him impatiently. "*Did* you drop it? Answer me!" And she shook him with violent eagerness.

Sawyer felt the lump on his forehead where the branch had struck him. He looked up. Broken limbs and the shower of leaves about him on the pavement attested to their passage. It had been a minor miracle that both of them survived the fall. So that dark cloud had masked an island? A floating island? He struck the pavement a tentative blow.

"Is it safe?" he asked nervously. "What holds it up?"

"What holds the sun up?" Nethe asked with exasperation. "How do I know? *Where is the Firebird?* Answer me quickly, before I kill you!"

It occurred to Sawyer belatedly that if she thought it gone forever, she would probably carry out her threat. "Treat me well and I'll tell you," he said rapidly. "I dropped it when we fell. I saw where it landed. You'll never find it without—"

She cast a quick glance around her in the dimness.

"Where did it fall?" she demanded. "Quick!"

"I won't tell you," he said.

Nethe's serpentine arm shot out and her hard hand cuffed him viciously across the side of the head. Her strength was tremendous. With the other hand she caught him as he fell, locked an iron grip on his forearm and twisted hard.

Between her shining teeth she said, "Answer me, Khom!"

The energy the Firebird had poured through him gave Sawyer strength to struggle. He shook his ringing head and lurched heavily away, putting his full weight on her grip to block her and swinging an edge-of-the-palm blow straight for the side of her neck, under the luminous earring.

Her flesh was inhuman, cool and hard. The blow jolted her a little, and she hissed in fury, twisting his arm up still farther so that the muscles creaked and he felt the joint give dangerously. The sweat sprang out on his forehead. He set his teeth and said in a thin, tight voice:

"Go on. Break it."

She glanced at him in surprise.

"I'm not a Khom," he said in a grating voice. "Break it. I won't talk. You can bargain all you like or you can kill me, but—"

She twisted harder. He caught his breath and struck futilely at her again, trying stubbornly to give with the twist to save his arm as long as he could. She would certainly have broken it, he thought in the next few seconds if a new element had not entered into their conflict.

A jagged stone sang through the air between them, flying out of nowhere, and struck Nethe across the forehead, sending her reeling.

Sawyer prudently dropped flat, massaging his freed arm

and searching the shadows with useless wariness. At the back of his mind was the knowledge that a stone that size should have knocked Nethe's brains out. He was quite certain, though it had happened almost too quickly to be sure, that at the instant of contact between missile and Isier head, a flash of brilliance had sprung out as though to cushion the impact. Presumably it had sprung from the Isier skull. So they really were invulnerable? That showed clearly why Nethe had been willing to risk the long drop through empty space to this floating islet. The fall that might have killed Sawyer had it not been for cushioning trees would have left the Isier woman unharmed.

There was no time to reflect about this, for Nethe had not touched the ground before tumult burst noisily from the trees. In the wake of the thrown rock a dark, indistinguishable horde of bodies hurtled upon them through the silver gloom.

Sawyer could not see them very clearly. He did not want to. There was a singular repulsiveness about their gait and the set of their heads on their squat shoulders. They were certainly not human. Even the Isier race seemed the very prototype of humanity by contrast. Yet they walked on two legs, and they could throw stones, and use artifacts. At least, Sawyer caught glints of long steely blades flashing among the mob that was overwhelming the pavement and surrounding him.

They moved with such preternatural speed that the musk-smelling creatures were all around Sawyer while he was still futilely gathering his wits and Nethe was picking herself up dizzily from the pavement. Sawyer felt strong, hard hands close on all his limbs at once. Struggling in vain, he was hauled upright with bonebreaking ease. They handled him as if he weighed no more than a straw man, and were no more breakable. It seemed sheer good luck that they did not bend his limbs backward, snapping every joint, as they put him on his feet.

He peered around him in the gloom. Were they tall or not tall? Their height seemed to keep changing, and in a moment he realized why. They had heads like turtles, shallow-skulled on thick, retractable necks that could squat down into their heavy shoulders or stretch high. It seemed to him that their long, terribly powerful limbs were boneless, for they moved with an incongruous grace.

They breathed a hot, musky breath in his face, pulling him from one to another, exchanging strangely musical grunts and trills in which pitch rather than words seemed to convey what little meaning moved through their shallow heads. In the dark their great pale eyes were like luminous jewels, perfectly empty, ringing him in.

One of them boomed resonantly in its throat, with a noise like drums echoing in a vault, and reached casually for Sawyer's head with both hands. Large, cold, musk-smelling, they closed around his face and ears, twisting. In a matter of seconds, he knew quite well, his head would part from his shoulders.

Between thumb and spread fingers of the great hand across his face, he saw Nethe, resisting capture with far more success than Sawyer, stemming as she did from a far stronger race.

He shouted to her, his voice muffled against the musky palm of the savage: "Nethe—Nethe!"

An explosion of sound and fury seemed to burst out among the knot of savages ringing Nethe in. He saw it only dimly, filtered between great spread fingers and blurred by his own swimming senses, but it looked as if Nethe had called upon some unfathomable source of incandescent power, for she whirled suddenly among her captors with a violence that sent them spinning. Her face lighted up with a blaze from within. Her eyes burned like lamps and she moved so fast she seemed to leave streaks of luminescence in the air around her.

At the same instant she lifted her voice in a cry like a struck gong. No human throat could have uttered a sound so resonant, so sustained, so clear. Sawyer had a mad notion that he could see the separate sound-waves of it spreading outward in luminous rings.

The savages responded surprisingly. Their hands fell free and Sawyer, wrenching his arms from the loosening grips that held them, massaged his aching neck with both hands and stared in bewilderment around the clearing. Every reptilian head was turned to Nethe, every pair of bright, empty, jewel-like eyes was fixed on her.

71

With great presence of mind Sawyer snatched a long knife from the nearest slack hand and plunged it up to the hilt in the deep chest of the savage before him.

"No!" Nethe called, from the other side of the group. "Don't waste your time—listen! Strip off that cloak. Throw it away. Quick, before it destroys you!"

Fumbling in dazed obedience at the fabric, Sawyer had one incredulous glimpse of the savage he had stabbed. The creature was watching Nethe in blurred fascination. It did not even look down when the blade entered its chest. One large paw came up and plucked the dagger out as if it had been a pin thrust through clothing. The savage chest showed no wound. The dark, reptilian flesh healed itself as the blade withdrew and there might never have been a stabbing at all, except that from the point of the blade two or three drops of golden, luminous blood dripped and vanished.

"Invulnerable!" Sawyer thought, a vague resentment stirring in him. "Everyone's invulnerable but me." And then he thought no more, for the cloak had begun to smoulder under his hands.

He got it off just in time. Like a Nessus-shirt it was turning to pure fire even as he tossed it, and the billowing folds settled down upon the pavement in a heap of flame, white-hot from hem to hood before it struck the ground.

The oval jewel-eyes of the savages followed its motion as if in hypnosis, every flattened head swinging round, every eye giving back a white flame of reflection. Nethe was forgotten. Sawyer was forgotten. They were moths around a flame, and it drew them irresistibly until their dark backs closing around the fire all but shut out its glow.

Sawyer had one brief, shuddering thought of what Nethe could have done to him with that shirt of Nessus any moment she chose, if his life hadn't been important to her at the time. How she had done it remained an enigma but the thing of utter blackness had in one instant become a thing of blinding light, growing brighter and brighter as the savages flocked around it, and apparently not actually burning for it did not consume itself. Whatever it fed on, it continued to blaze higher, and the savages continued to surge excitedly around it, more of them appearing out of the woods at every flare of the cloak.

On the other side of that mindlessly phototropic crowd he caught a flash of Nethe's lantern earrings as she dodged futilely, trying to get to him, and he came back to the realization of danger with a start. She had saved him for her own purposes, but it mattered little whether he was dismembered fatally by a savage or an Isier, and dismemberment would certainly be his end if she caught him.

He whirled and ran. . . .

VIII

BEYOND THE FRINGE of trees a range of dark hills rose against the silver mist of the sky. Sawyer labored stumbling up the slope, with no clear plan except to put space between himself and Nethe. He did not forget that this was an island, improbably drifting in space. He watched the ground underfoot suspiciously, and presently, between two hills, caught a glimpse of low-lying silver fog that looked like the brink of creation.

It was. He came out on the height of the next hill and pulled up sharply, seizing the trunk of a leaning tree to steady himself. He and the tree leaned together over the abyss. This was the shore of space. Eddies of mist lapped against the sheer drop at his very toes. The tree dangled its roots as a more familiar tree had done far above. Sawyer could see them swaying gently outward below, which probably meant the island was in motion.

Clasping the tree, he leaned out farther, shuddering, and saw that what he had from above taken to be dark clouds were actually islands, many of them, each carrying a cumulus over its center, drifting slowly in long, descending festoons between the upper world and that far-off, shadowy, mysterious world below. Almost like stairsteps, he thought. If you watched your chance, you might climb up from island to island as they rose and fell in their drifting, until, from the topmost, you could reach Khom'ad—

73

Was that why the city gates were guarded? Did they expect attack?

He glanced up, and caught his breath as he saw that the vast, impending thundercloud which was the under-side of Khom'ad glowed crimson and flickered with glancing white flashes and gleams. It looked like the end of the world. Then he realized that what he saw was nothing more sinister than the burning cloak, which must have become quite a respectable holocaust by now, sending down strong reflections from the overhang of the world above.

He saw something else, too, when he looked back. Two twinkling points of light were moving rapidly toward him up the ravine. Nethe had found her quarry. Sawyer clasped the tree and urged Providence to remember him. For he was quite literally between the devil and the deep. Nethe cut off retreat, and the abyss was a long way down.

Nethe saw him, silhouetted against the silver sky. She laughed in triumph, a clear, strong, musical laugh.

"One last chance," she called to him as she came. "If you tell me where the Firebird is before I get to you, I'll let you live."

Sawyer looked down. He dangled a tentative foot over the void.

"All right," he told her clearly. "That's close enough. Stop right there. If you've got anything to say, I can hear you. But say it from where you are, because I'd rather jump than let you kill me."

Nethe laughed, but a little hesitantly. She slowed, and then came on. Sawyer leaned far out. Rocks crumbled underfoot and rattled across the edge.

Nethe paused uncertainly.

"Be sensible, Khom," she urged. "You can't stand there forever. I'll get you when you give out. You have to sleep. You—"

"I'm not a Khom," Sawyer said in a patient voice. "You can't order me around and you may as well get used to it. I know where the Firebird fell. And not on this island, incidentally." He glanced down and wondered if he really did see the motion of crowding figures on the next lower land below.

"Tell me and I'll spare your life," Nethe offered, taking a tentative forward step. Casually Sawyer kicked another stone over the edge. She stopped.

"I might tell you," he said, "if you made it worth my while. Otherwise I'll just wait until the island grounds against the mainland. I can see they float. I can imagine what the gates of Khom'ad are guarded against. They must be expecting an attack. What made you drop us both on this island, anyhow? Didn't you know it was crawling with these savages?"

"I didn't mean to drop either of us on *this* one," Nethe told him with some asperity. "If you hadn't made such a fuss about falling we'd have struck a smaller island. It was right under you when you first dropped. But you had to hang on to that root and argue. So—"

"So that was the plan," Sawyer murmured. "Drop Alper far enough to kill him and then loot the corpse. Well, now you've caught a Tartar. What do you offer me if I give up the Firebird?"

"Death if you don't!" Nethe cried, and surged forward three eager steps. "So you have it? On you?"

Sawyer kicked another stone over the edge.

"Imagine that's me," he said. "With the Firebird." She paused reluctantly. "No, I haven't got it on me," he went on. "You know that, you searched me, didn't you? Besides, if I had it do you think I'd stay here? I'd use it. I'd—I'd open up the Gateway and go right back where I came from."

"You fool, you couldn't open the Gateway," Nethe said contemptuously.

"Alper did," Sawyer reminded her.

"There's more to opening a door than waving a key around," she told him aloofly. "If I hadn't already unlocked the Gateway to send Klai through, the Firebird wouldn't have had any effect at all except to call the real Firebirds down the tunnel."

"What are real Firebirds?" Sawyer inquired with interest.

Before she could answer, a new sound began to shake the air and both looked up quickly. The deep, heavy clangor of a great bell from somewhere above began to beat wildly through the abyss. Some resonance in its pitch made the island shiver slightly at every peal.

"They've seen the islands rising," Nethe said, her face turned upward and away and her mask seeming to regard Sawyer with a disinterested stare. "It's the Khom alarm-bell."

While the echoes still rang, a second bell, farther off, took up the signal, and far away, at the very verge of hearing, a third began heavily to toll. Sawyer imagined the mobilization at the city gates, and he hoped the tuba-shaped weapons were better fit to deal with the savages than a knife through the chest had been.

"Are they really invulnerable?" he asked Nethe. "The savages, I mean?"

"The Sselli? To most things, yes. Like us."

"Then you are vulnerable too?"

"Not to you, Khom." She laughed and turned back to him, her eyes baleful. "All living things are vulnerable—to something. Only the Goddess can unleash the weapon that could destroy an Isier. Don't worry. The Sselli won't get far. Do you think a little band that size could stand against the Isier?"

Sawyer looked down at the circling swarm of islands upon which he had thought he saw the motion of living things. Perhaps a small band could be driven back, then, but not a large one? He strained his eyes through the dimness, which was beginning now to brighten with reflections from the upper world, long shafts of red and crimson streaming downward past this island and touching with a sort of false sunrise color the rising lands below.

The rock shivered under him in answer to the wild timbre of alarm-bells in the city. He thought of Jericho and the shivering walls. It might have been coincidence, or it might have been a faint premonitory tremor that made him think "Jericho!" for in the next instant a still, small, far-off quiver, terribly familiar, moved between his brain and his skull. . . .

"Alper!" he thought. "Awake. The bells—did they rouse him? Now he's sitting up, looking around the cell, trying to remember." He could picture it very clearly. "Now he's thought of me. Now he has his hand in his pocket, feeling for the transceiver control. Now he's found the note. . . ."

He could imagine Alper struggling up in the glass cell, his face dark with anger, hand in pocket, finding there the unexpected crackle of paper. In a moment Sawyer would know if his note was going to save him. His life was in Alper's pocket. Alper could kill him with the motion of one finger as dead as if they stood in the same room with a loaded gun between them. If anger made Alper's hand clench before he fully took in the import of the note—

"Alper!" Sawyer said sharply. "Do you hear me? Listen!"

The tremor shivered in his brain for an endless moment. Then very softly it ceased to be. Alper was listening.

"What is the Firebird?" Sawyer asked distinctly. And he could almost imagine that at the crown of his skull the transceiver quivered with listening intentness. That question of all questions Alper would most want to hear answered. To make the situation perfectly clear, he added, "What is it, Nethe?"

"The key," Nethe said impatiently. "The key between worlds. Also, it's the lens of the Well. Lens? Shutter? I don't know your language well enough. There may be no equivalent. What does it matter to you, anyhow? You can't use it. Let me warn you—don't try. You could unlock powers even the Isier can't control. Tell me where it is and I—I promise you safety."

"Ha," Sawyer said, and swung his foot over the abyss. "That's the hollowest promise I ever heard." He laughed. He felt a little light-headed. For the moment at least both Alper and Nethe were in his hands. While the moment lasted he meant to make the most of it.

Nethe's eyes blazed. "Listen, Khom! My life depends on getting the Firebird back. The Goddess hates me. In three more days she must give up her place to me. It was my plan to wait in your world until the three days were over and she automatically lost the Double Mask to me.

"But you and your friend Alper spoiled that plan. Through your clumsiness I was drawn through into Khom'ad without the Firebird. For that I'll kill Alper when I get to him. It was dangerous enough here in Khom'ad for me with the

77

Firebird. But at least, while I held it, I could escape whenever I chose. There are gates to a long, strange pathway we Isier travel, through many worlds and forms. With the Firebird, I can pass them. Without it, I'm helpless.

"The Goddess' guards are watching for me, and if they catch me I'll have to face her at the Ceremony of the Unsealing. One of us will die. If I have the Firebird, I'll win it. If I don't—"

"Maybe I'd better get in touch with the Goddess, then," Sawyer said cheerfully. "Alper, are you listening?" This last was *sotto voce*.

"Khom!" Nethe said furiously. "Animal!"

"Stand back," Sawyer warned her. "I'm perfectly willing to bargain. For instance, could you send me back to the world I came from?" He added hastily, "With Alper, of course. And Klai too, if she wants to go."

"Klai is being hunted by the guards now. She'll go as a sacrifice at the Unsealing. But you I could send back. And Alper too. Now give me the Firebird and—"

"Not so fast," Sawyer advised her. "What can you do for me the Goddess can't?"

"I can let you live!" Nethe said violently, and surged forward a little without actually leaving her place. "The Goddess knows nothing! Nothing! Only I could send you back."

"Interesting, if true," Sawyer murmured, and turned his head to glance for a second down the abyss where the islands rose and fell. Light from the fire was beginning to touch the uppermost, and on these a vague stirring of motion among the trees was visible.

"If you make it clear enough," he said, "I might be persuaded. Go on, convince me." It was in his mind that with Alper listening—and he hoped Alper was—something might emerge which the old man's trained brain could make sense of even if Sawyer's could not.

Nethe gave him a long, hating look and said, "The Isier are gods. Why should I talk to you, animal? No, no—I will. I'll make it clear. Once we were mortal, long ago. Never human, like you lower orders, but mortal. Until we made our great discovery and our great change. That happened a thousand years ago on another world—the world you see below us. It turns inside the vast outer shell which is Khom'ad, and these islands rise and sink on great gravitational currents flowing between the Under-Shell and the world above.

"In the ancient days our wise men made the Well of the Worlds, and after that we became gods. It worked a change in us so that our appearance—altered. Our bodies altered both inside and out, and yet we were the same. I can only explain it by a thing I learned on your world—the creation of isotopes is very like what the Well did for us. We became isotopes of our earlier selves. And the isotopes were gods, except for one thing—we need energy.

"All the power we need we draw out of the Well. It gives us immortality. We can resist all bodily harm, we heal instantly, we never eat or drink or sleep. I'll tell you how the Well works, as nearly as I can, and then perhaps even your limited animal mind can understand the danger in the Firebird.

"There are many worlds in creation. Many states of matter. You know that? You know your sun, for instance, differs from the solid Earth? Well, there are many such states, far more than you would ever dream. Worlds of a vapor, for instance, attenuated not necessarily in *space*. States of matter inconceivable to you but no less real than your own planet.

"Khom'ad is a world of such other-matter. Your sun and worlds are invisible to us, as we are to you. Just as there are colors beyond the two ends of the visible spectrum, so there are states of matter above hydrogen and below the transuranic elements you know.

"But though these worlds and stars are invisible to us, they're accessible through the Well. As your sun radiates energy to your world, so we draw energy from the vast seas of other-space. The Well drains it as we drift and the energy is radiated to us as we choose to take it, much or little, according to the need of the individual Isier. You have the transmission of energy through the air in your own world. We receive it in a similar way, regulating our intake as we need."

"Transformers," Sawyer murmured. "Built in, I suppose. An X-ray photo of an Isier ought to be very informative. I wonder if you've got coils of wire inside. Never mind. Don't tell me. You haven't come to the Firebird yet."

"The Firebird is the energy-control from the Well. It belongs in the Well. It should be there now. It was stolen—" Nethe paused and then said firmly, "The Goddess stole it. And then all our troubles began. You see, we drifted near your world, which happens to have rich deposits of uranium near its pole. Our world's pole is the Well. It is, incidentally, our south pole, which helps to explain what happened when the Firebird was—stolen.

"The uranium made your world too strong a power-source for us. I think there's a great deal your people don't understand yet about what you call fissionable substances. And not uranium alone.

"Normally when we touch so rich a source of power the Firebird-control in the Well closes its wings and dies for awhile. This makes the Well go dead until we pass beyond danger. Otherwise the Well might drink up too much energy and burn out not only itself, but all the Isier too."

"A circuit-breaker," Sawyer said. "I see. What happened?"

"When your world drifted near ours, and the Firebird closed its wings, the Goddess happened to be alone by the Well. She saw her chance to lift the little control out of its place. This was one of the few times when it could be safely touched or moved. Instantly, when the control was lifted out of its place, the two worlds flashed together and sealed in an unbreakable fusion, because of the terribly powerful magnetic attraction between north pole and south. They'll never be separated until the Firebird is put back into the Well.

"So now the two worlds are locked together. But the Well is dead. The Isier receive less and less energy. They don't understand why. Only the Goddess and I know, and *she* has no idea where the Firebird really is. There have been times when our world drifted through other-space in regions where energy-sources were low. Then too our power flowed feebly. In times like that we have to feed sacrifices into the Well. That replenishes our energy until we drift out of the dead spaces into a place of stars again. The Isier think this is what's happening now.

80

"But it isn't. The energy will never flow again until the Firebird goes back into the Well. Meanwhile we offer sacrifices to keep the Isier alive and immortal. It gives us energy, but not enough. Disastrous things have happened. When an Isier uses up more energy than he possesses—something changes in him. I spoke of the parallel with isotopic elements. I think something very like that happens here. An Isier discharges more energy than he has and—and changes."

Sawyer thought of the familiar three-stage isotopic change from uranium 238 through neptunium to plutonium, the complex rearrangement of charges and masses that can take an isotope of uranium around a cycle through plutonium and bring it out uranium again, but 235 three points down the scale from its start.

"It happens because they're unstable," he murmured. "Neptunium discharges an electron and turns into—oh, never mind. Go on. What does the Isier turn into?"

Nethe gave him a supicious glance. "He seems to—to vaporize in a cloud of heat. And then, much later, he returns as you saw, through the Ice-Hall. That was what I meant when I said we travel by a long, strange pathway, through more than one form. What happens in that interval no one could tell you, for no one remembers."

She moved forward one impatient pace.

"Now you know the whole story. Will you give me the Firebird, or shall I make you jump?"

"What about these savages?" Sawyer inquired, anxious to get every element laid before the listening Alper.

"They're part of the punishment the Goddess must suffer for stealing the Firebird. The trouble will go on until the Firebird is replaced. I got it away from her. When I'm Goddess I'll put it back and the troubles of my people will all be over."

"You could give her back the Firbird," Sawyer suggested. "Why did she do such a stupid thing, anyhow? She was Goddess to start with. Or *was* it she who stole it, Nethe?"

"Of course it was," Nethe declared rapidly. "She wanted power, more power than the Well would give her. Why should I hand the Firebird back and let her keep the Mask

81

and Robe? When I'm Goddess it'll be time enough to restore the Firebird. Let her suffer her own punishment."

Sawyer looked at her thoughtfully. It seemed perfectly clear to him who had really snatched the Firebird from the Well. He hoped Alper was listening. He wondered if the Goddess had questioned him yet, and how much Alper would see fit to pass on from this conversation, if it were possible to communicate at all.

"I still don't understand what the real Firebirds are," he said. "What do they do? What's the connection between the real Firebirds and the—the little symbol?"

"I won't tell you that," Nethe said, with a flash of brilliant anger. "Go ahead and jump if you want to. I will tell you this much—they feed on the energy in the uranium at your world's pole. They can drink energy from the Khom, too. They could drink from you. Perhaps, in time, they will." She gave him a dangerous look.

"What would happen," Sawyer inquired, "if the Goddess knew you had the Firebird?"

"Perhaps she does. But she doesn't intend to let anyone else know the Firebird's gone from the Well. The Well is her trust—her charge. Do you suppose she would want to advertise the fact that she allowed—that she stole the Firebird?"

Sawyer grinned. He felt quite sure now who had really stolen that strange talisman. Perhaps Nethe read his face, for she went on:

"Would you like to go to her with your story? The first thing the Goddess would force you to do is reveal where you've hidden the Firebird. She has powers I haven't—yet. And the second thing she would do would be to seal your mouth forever, so you could never reveal that the Goddess had failed her trust. She wears the Double Mask, and she intends to keep on wearing it—by killing me, if she can, at the Unsealing. And if I die, the Goddess will make no bargains with a Khom like you. Why do you suppose I didn't simply wait for you outside the Temple?"

"For Alper, you mean," Sawyer said. "Well, why didn't you? What were you afraid of?"

"The soldiers of the Goddess, of course," Nethe said. "I've disobeyed the summons to the Unsealing. I intend to keep on disobeying it as long as I can hide, but where can I hide from the Goddess in Khom'ad? Nowhere, for long, without the Firebird to open a Gate past which even the Goddess can't follow me."

"The Gate to Earth?" Sawyer asked.

Nethe hestitated for an instant.

"Somewhere else, then?" Sawyer went on speculatively, watching her. "Back in the uranium mine, you intended to take Klai through the Gate to question her—but I don't think it was to Khom'ad. Then we all were sucked through into that ice-hall, so. . . ." Sawyer paused, nodded once, and continued briskly, "So perhaps that's a necessary way-station to wherever you'd intended to take Klai. But you couldn't finish the trip without the Firebird. The current in the ice-hall carried you away—carried all of us away except Alper, who had the Firebird then."

"Never mind that," Nethe said impatiently. "You understand now that I'm desperate. The city's alive with soldiers searching for Khom sacrifices—during the Unsealing, the Well drinks up many lives. And outside the city, the Goddess has ways of finding me—so now I intend to get the Firebird, or you can jump." She took a long, smooth forward step. "Make up your mind, animal. Is it yes or no?"

Sawyer glanced down again into the swimming abysses below, combed now by long, slanting shafts of reflection from the fire that glowed just beyond the hill. He had been watching considerable activity growing and changing down there, where the rising islands floated in the light of the false sunrise from above.

"Just a moment, Nethe," he said. "One little matter you haven't considered yet. I don't know if you realize it, but your fire has become quite an attraction among the—Sselli, you called them? I think there's going to be some excitement in Khom'ad very soon now. Climb that rock beside you and you can see. Not too near, though! Careful! I can always jump."

She hissed at him scornfully, put her foot in a pocket of rock and climbed until she could see what he meant. Then she sucked her breath in with a sound of consternation.

In the ruddy glow of the fire reflecting downward from

Khom'ad's underside, the floating lands were alive with great hordes of climbing Sselli, clambering swiftly upward toward the glow, leaping from isle to rising isle, springing the dangling roots and swarming up them like creatures under a spell of hypnotized fascination. Their blank, lifted eyes reflected red and flat in the light which drew them on.

At this moment a violent shock made the ground jump like a spurred horse under Sawyer's feet. Nethe swore in Isier and slid helpless down the rock to which she had been clinging. Only Swayer's instinctive embrace of his tree saved him from pitching to destruction over the cliff As it was, he struck his head painfully against the trunk and saw stars for a moment.

Then the island under him swung ponderously around in a full quarter-turn. Something brushed his face with a familiar network and he looked up in time to receive a moist smack in the cheek from a dripping tree-root. The island had risen until it all but touched the underhang of Khom'ad, and the roots which were dripping now with rain from the upper world brushed the tree-tops of the island.

Overhead, floating like the gates of heaven, loomed through darkness and rain the high iron doors and the granite wall of Khom's gateway. The doors were opening. The bells rang wildly all through the city now.

Sawyer clasped his tree and watched.

IX

A WATERFALL of human figures was pouring over the lip of the upper world. The light of the reflecting fire caught on steel tubes and coils of the mysterious Khom weapons, flashed on long blades like bayonets. The dark torrent glittered as it leaped, and the island shook with the impact of the falling human torrent.

They were shouting as they came.

The deep booming cries of the savages answered like inhuman echoes. Reptilian heads sunk flatly between their shoulders, long arms swinging, knives flashing, they surged forward to meet the Khom.

84

Above the roar of the human battlecries and the deep bellows of the Sselli, a great, clear, belling shout rang like a golden gong, struck three times. A second cry, and then a third, joined in the ringing sound, three voices that overlapped like ripples in a pool. And over the brink of the human waterfall as it poured between the gates, three god-like figures came.

Three tall Isiers waded head and shoulders above the dark human tide. Above the heads of the Khom they swung three great whips of flame, crackling and snapping like leashed lightning. They were shouting, in the voices of angry angels, deep and golden and terrible.

Here at last, Sawyer thought, came something that might have a chance against the Sselli.

At the first sound of those golden shouts, Nethe writhed around anxiously, hissing with anger. She gave Sawyer a hot, baleful look, hesitated, took a step toward him. Very quickly he turned too, leaned perilously over the abyss, and said across his shoulder, "You haven't got a chance. I'll jump and you know it."

In the way she lashed around in an agony of indecision to look again at the oncoming Isier, Sawyer was startled to see a curious likeness to the motion of the Sselli, the same strong, sinuous, violent ripple of El Greco distortions.

"Don't think you've won!" she spat at him, her great eyes luminous with rage. "I've told you things too dangerous for you to know. You won't get away! I'll—" She bit off the rest of the words, smiled at him fiercely, and then with one ripple of sinuous motion hurled herself sidewise off the rock and vanished between two low hills away from the direction of the fighting.

He strained his eyes among the shadows, seeing nothing. Perhaps she had really gone. And, of course, perhaps not. He took a few cautious steps inland, watching the battle.

The first ranks of the human waterfall poured forward. In a long, sinuous wave the Sselli leaped to meet them, and the shock of their impact made the island stagger.

The Isier were wading through the turmoil, their whips of fire crackling and coiling brilliantly in the air before them. Their great voices rang above the deep-throated roars of the Sselli and the wild human shouts and cries. Above it all the iron alarm-bells still rolled forth their clangor on the reverberating air. The half-smothered light of the blazing cloak shot low shafts of light between upper world and island to illuminate the battle from below. It was like the light of hell-fire glowing up from the nether pit.

Sawyer saw the foremost Isier and a Sselli come face to face in the wild, tossing turmoil of the battle. A spark of hatred seemed to leap out between them. The eyes of the savage blazed and upon the Isier's godlike face a fury of disdain burned incandescently. He swung his fiery whip high, brought it curling down to wrap the monstrous, reptilian being in a coil of lightning.

The Sselli howled, reeled, fell . . . but it did not die. Sawyer watched eagerly. He saw the creature sink, hesitate, then shake its flat head and struggle up again, sluggish and dazed but still fighting.

There was a rattle and scuffling among the stones between two hills, and a human head wearing a pointed cap came into silhouette, paused, shouted something and came pelting full-tilt down the little ravine toward Sawyer, waving eagerly. Sawyer jumped back to his tree, ready to immolate himself if this were a trick.

The running Khom burst out into the reflecting light of the fire and dashed panting toward Sawyer, still waving. He was gasping out a single syllable, over and over, but too indistinctly to mean anything. Sawyer hesitated.

Then dimly recognition began to dawn. That pointed cap. That dark face. He had last seen them receding with frightful speed down the wrong end of a telescope as he fell through the air-well—

The man pulled up sharply when he saw the sheer drop of the cliff beside which Sawyer stood. He got his breath, nodded rapidly, and said, "Klai! Klai!" For one wild moment the word meant nothing. Then Sawyer sprang forward, shook the man by the shoulders and echoed, "Klai? Klai?" in senseless repetition.

The man grinned broadly, nodded many times and seized Sawyer by the arm, urging him away from the edge. Sawyer allowed himself to be pulled toward the fighting, though he kept a wary lookout all around him. His mind was clicking bits of logic into place. Uselessly he spoke in English to his excited guide.

"You followed me from the prison," he said. "You saw me fall and the islands rise, with the savages on them. Was it you who sounded the alarm? Are you taking me to Klai now?"

The little man said, "Klai," many times over, nodded, urged Sawyer to greater speed. He paused on the height of a low hill above the battle. Clearly he had hoped to make his way across that struggling turmoil and up through the city gates. Equally clearly, no such thing was possible now, with the fight spread so widely.

Sawyer glanced speculatively toward the dark overhang of the great looming continent that floated above them. The island had pressed itself up close beneath the shell of the upper world. Perhaps two-thirds of it thrust out free and clear into the space before the city gates, like a gigantic doorstep leading into infinity.

In the upper world, rain still fell. The part of the island which had undershot the upper world was sheltered, but through that roof, not far away, a shaft of rain drove downward slantingly in intermittent gusts. There was an opening there, in the crust of the upper world. Sawyer thought he knew that opening.

He said, "Come on," and seized his companion by the arm. The little man resisted unexpectedly, plucked Sawyer's sleeve and pointed. Sawyer turned to look.

They stood just below the crest of the hill. Below them, across the broad, broken pavement, the fighting raged under gusts of fitful rain. On the far side Sawyer saw Nethe swaying between the trees, peering out at them and up, her face white with excitement and rage. The earrings glinted across her cheeks. She kept the trees between herself and the striding Isier, and her eyes burned upon the hilltop that hid Sawyer.

"She knows we're here," Sawyer said uselessly, in English. "We've got to get away before she can work around toward us. Come on!" But he did not move. Something very curious about Nethe's eyes had struck him suddenly. He stood for an instant staring down in fascination, and a strange new idea began to stir formlessly in his mind.

For by sheer chance one of the savages had glanced blindly up toward Sawyer in the instant that Nethe lifted her own face. And Sawyer saw its eyes. . . .

They were the same eyes. Large, oval, lucent as jewels, the same shape, the same set and angle in the head. The Sselli's were blank as two clear gems. But except for the fiery mind behind one pair of eyes and the total mindlessness behind the other, they might have been the same eyes reflected in two differing faces.

Sawyer's guide tugged at him again. Reluctantly, dazed with the strange idea that seemed to mean nothing, he turned away. And once more something stopped him. Something else spectacular was happening down below.

An Isier, wading forward like an angel scourging demons before him, came stalking through the tides of human allies, swinging his whip of flame. A flung knife shot from the hand of a Sselli and flashed toward him. The Isier smiled with godlike scorn. The knife rang upon his ice-robed chest as if upon a wall of steel. A flash of pure energy seemed to gleam between the blade and the Isier. The knife fell harmlessly away—

But the Isier stood as if frozen. For a long, immobile second he stood there, his face suddenly blank, his eyes glazing. Then a burst of shimmering heat sprang out around him in a halo that made the battle-scenes behind him quiver when glimpsed through that haze.

The next instant he was gone.

Sselli and Khom alike leaped back as if scorched from that fading bright spot where he had stood. They looked blankly at each other, shook their heads dazedly, and then the battle swept forward and closed like water over the spot where the Isier had been.

When an Isier uses up more energy than he possesses, he seems to—to vaporize. . . . So Nethe had said in her long, reluctant talk beside the brink of the island.

Shaking his own head, bewildered by the ideas that were beginning to take shape in his mind about the Isier, Sawyer turned away. He had one small errand to perform before he

88

returned to the city. And it would have to be a secret errand, even from his guide.

"Come along," he said, leading the little man firmly away from the battle-ground. "We're going upstairs by the trap-door."

Rain still fell through the familiar air-well down which Sawyer had fallen. The hole floated in the world's overhang, ten feet above the island. The well-remembered tap-root trailed downward upon the ground, dragging its broken end.

"You first," Sawyer said, making appropriate gestures. The little man leaped for the root, shinnied rapidly upward and scrambled out of sight over the edge.

Sawyer followed, more slowly, scanning the damp soil he passed with an anxious eye. It seemed too good to be true, but there was the familiar burrow with the rock blocking it. He exhaled deeply, pulled out the rock, dropped it, thrust his fist into the hole and in another moment felt the precious golden bar of the Firebird throbbing warmly against his hand.

He dropped the terrible, wonderful, dangerous thing into his pocket and went rapidly up the rope. The little man waited grinning at the top to help him over the edge.

Twice in their devious, rapid course through the dark streets of the city. Sawyer's guide paused, drew back into a doorway and whistled softly in warning to Sawyer. The city was alive with excited Khom, but this little man had a knowledge of byways so complete that they never had to cross a lighted thoroughfare.

He had a sixth sense about pursuit, too, for the second time he pulled Sawyer into hiding they saw the flash of white robes behind them, dodging out of sight, and a faint, luminous glow that was almost certainly Nethe's earrings.

"So that was her idea," Sawyer thought. "She had to hide when the Goddess's soldiers started that beachhead attack on the island. But now? Maybe she thinks she can track me to the Firebird." He shut his hand on the warm glow in his pocket, thinking, "She didn't see me get it when I climbed the root. She couldn't have, or she'd have caught up with me by now. No, she's still following hoping I'll give myself away."

The little guide tapped Sawyer softly on the shoulder, tinkered for an instant with the door in whose shadow they hid, then pushed it soundlessly open and led the way through total darkness down rickety stairs and out a low window in the back. They plunged into another alley and set off at a rapid trot.

It occurred to Sawyer as he ran that he had better post Alper on current events or he might receive a jolt from the transceiver when it would do the most harm. So, in a whisper, he talked eerily to the distant, unseen enemy who controlled his life while he ran through an unknown city at a stranger's heels, toward an unknown goal.

That goal turned out to be a cul-de-sac alley, dark and smelling not unpleasantly of hay and stabled animals. Sawyer's companion rattled his nails in a brisk code on a half-seen door. Two Khom came up quietly out of nowhere, peered into their faces, exchanged murmurs and withdrew. The door opened. Quickly Sawyer and his guide slipped through.

A lantern burning some pungent-smelling oil swung from a low rafter, its motion making the shadows seem to rock dizzily. The heads of leopard-spotted ponies nodded drowsily over their stalls along both walls. Under the lantern reddish chickens scratched and pecked at the chaff-strewn floor. And all around the walls one simultaneous motion of turning bodies, turning heads, quickly narrowing eyes, greeted the newcomers.

The stable was packed with Khom. They sat three deep along the stalls, clogged the corners, swung their legs over the hay-fringed edges of the mows above the ponies. Their eyes glinted in the lantern-light and they held themselves alertly poised, ready for any trouble that came, from any source.

At the far end of the stable, on a bale of hay, a plump old man sat with a striped cat on his knees. And beside him, fast asleep on a spread blue cloak, lay Klai with her hand under her cheek, smudges of smoke and ash on her face, and her pretty teeth showing a little under her lip.

The old man shook her gently. Her eyes came open instantly, deep blue and blank with sleep. Then she scrambled up, cried, "Sawyer!" and stumbled forward, still dazed from slumber but smiling, reaching out her hands.

He took them eagerly. It was tremendously consoling to see a familiar face again and speak English to it. But she was, at first, babbling out phrases in her own tongue. He said, "Wait a minute! Hello!" and she laughed, shook her head with confusion, and changed over to English, though strange phrases kept tumbling into it in her excitement.

"You're safe?" she demanded. "Am I still dreaming. Are you all right? I got you into trouble you didn't bargain for when I dragged you into my problems, didn't I? I'm awfully sorry. I—"

"Keep it in English!" Sawyer broke in. "I can't understand Khom! We're all in trouble and we'll have to help each other out." He touched the soot-stain on her cheek. "What's been happening to you?"

"The Isier guards came," she said simply. "We knew they would, of course. They burned grandfather's house and we just got away in time. They're still hunting for me. Probably they'd have found me already if this attack on the city hadn't started. Were you involved in that? Do tell me what's been happening to you!"

A crisp phrase from behind her made Klai turn. The old man was smiling at them, but his blue eyes stayed cool and wary. He stroked the stable cat with unvaried smoothness, but what he said made Klai pull herself together and turn Sawyer to face the old man.

"Zatri is his name," she said. "He's my grandfather, and he's a wonderful man. He says there isn't much time to waste. I told him about the Firebird and what Nethe said back there on the steps, before the Goddess came. The Firebird's something we don't know about, but grandfather thinks it may be very important. He wants to know what's been happening, but there may not be time for much talk. The Sselli are beginning to swarm up into the city, and we may have fighting in the streets too close for comfort. Grandfather hopes you may have some information we can use."

"What sort of information?" Sawyer asked.

Klai repeated the question and the old man's eyes gleamed as he leaned forward, speaking in urgent syllables.

"For a thousand years," Klai translated soberly when he finished, "the Isier have enslaved our people. We aren't allowed freedom of any kind, not even freedom to think or to learn. To the Isier we're simply animals. Grandfather thinks this may be our chance to put an end to their rule.

"He wants you to know he wouldn't have risked the lives of his men when they rescued me from the Isier, not even to save his own grandchild, if he hadn't hoped I'd brought back some sort of information we could use, from wherever I'd been. Well, I didn't. But he thinks maybe you might."

"Wait a minute," Sawyer said. "Tell him I'm with him if he wants to make trouble for the Isier. I got into this in the first place to stop the looting of uranium from Fortuna. I know a lot more about that than I did. I want to get back to Earth and finish my job. I'd like to stay alive, too. I'd just as soon you did." He smiled at her. "But I wouldn't interfere with the Isier now, even if I could. Without them, who's going to prevent the Sselli from killing us all? Have the Khom any defense against them?"

She shook her head, gave him a troubled glance. "From what I hear, not even the Isier can actually destroy them. They seem to be a little—oh, overawed, terrified—by the Isier. But not when they're in a frenzy, like right now. I don't know *what's* going to happen."

"I wish I knew a little more about those savages," Sawyer said. "Surely you've developed some way to deal with them, or you'd all be dead."

"But they're new!" Klai said. "They only began to trouble us when the Isier Well went dry. We Khom aren't supposed to know about that, of course, but my grandfather was a Temple slave for a long, long time, and he knows all sorts of secret listening posts in the Temple. We even know why the Isier fear the Sselli.

"Sselli means—well, younger brother, but with a strong sense of hatred and rivalry. The Isier say the Goddess committed some frightful sin in allowing the Well to die. Now the whole race is being punished. The Isier originated down below in the lower world, the Under-Shell. It's forbidden land. Nobody ever goes there. But soon after the Well died, lights began to shine down there, and then the Sselli started to wander up the floating islands and make a lot of trouble. They're invulnerable, like the Isier themselves. The theory is that a new race of potential gods is being reared in the Isier homeland, to take over when they're strong enough. So naturally, the Isier hate and fear the Sselli."

"But they don't look like the Isier," Sawyer complained. "How could they evolve into—"

"I know," Klai broke in. "It puzzles the Isier, too. And yet in many ways they *are* like. Remember this, too. The Fire-birds began on Earth when the Sselli began here. And you never see the Firebirds in Khom'ad. They seem to exist only on Earth."

"At the other end of the Well," Sawyer said. "Now that's very interesting. There must be some connection. The three forms of life *must* be three facets of a single problem. But—"

The belling cry of an Isier from close outside broke sharply into his words.

For an instant the deepest silence dwelt upon the stable, broken only by the crunching of the ponies in their stalls, and from far off a rising noise of battle. The Sselli had not been audible when Sawyer first got here. That must mean they had gained a foothold on the upper world and were carrying the battle straight into the heart of the Isier-ruled city. If the Isier have weapons, he thought grimly, they'd better start limbering them up.

The silence held for half a minute. Then there was a sudden outburst of scuffling, stamping, ringing cries from Isier throats, and above it a fierce, wild scream that Sawyer thought could come from one throat only.

"Nethe!" he said, and whirled toward the door.

Zatri, moving faster than seemed possible, was at his very elbow when he got the door open. The old man snapped an order and someone put out the lamp. Then there was a great surge toward the neck of the alley to see what the trouble was.

Nethe was the trouble. A little way off down the street Sawyer saw her familiar figure, the luminous earrings swinging wildly, struggling between two tall Isier who were carrying her serenely forward down the street toward the Temple. She writhed and fought and spat violent bursts of speech at them. They did not seem to hear. The backward-facing masks of all three turned a blank, uninterested stare at the little knot of humans who watched from the alley.

"She must have followed us after all," Sawyer said. "Well, that takes care of Nethe. I wonder what the Goddess will do?"

"Force her into the Unsealing ceremony," Klai said, from a prudent shelter behind him. "And that will be the end of one or the other of them. But whichever wins, the Isier rule will go on the way it always has, unless we find a way to fan this trouble higher. Come back. We've got a lot of planning to do."

"All right," Sawyer said. "But tell me one thing. What the devil are those masks for?"

A voice from the street corner just beyond their alley said calmly:

"That's an interesting question, my boy. Look what I've brought you."

Sawyer knew that voice. The thick organ-tones could belong to one man only. He turned and said, "Alper!"

The ponderous figure of Alper moved toward them. He was walking effortlessly still, so the power the Firebird gave him had not yet waned, but there was already a suggestion of a drag to his gait, and his heavy figure stooped a little.

In each hand he carried a pale, smiling, blind-eyed Isier mask.

X

ZATRI SAT DOWN again upon his haybale throne. The watchful Khom lined the walls, patient and alert in the swinging shadows cast by the relit lamp. Alper stood under it, his heavy head sunk a little, his big legs braced, taking in the group with quick, cold, purposeful glances. Outside, in the night, the noises of battle were much louder. The dull booming of the Sselli, the Younger Brothers, echoed down the narrow streets of Khom'ad, and the shouts and screams of their human opponents, and the ringing calls of the Isier. Alper jerked his head toward the noise.

"They'll have to speed up the Ceremony of the Unsealing,"

94

he said to Sawyer. "I've talked to the Goddess. With these"
—he shook the two smiling masks—"it was perfectly simple
to communicate. Most of the time you and Nethe were
having your little consultation on the island, I was relaying
the story to the Goddess. Luckily, she couldn't understand
you. You weren't wearing a mask, and it takes two of them
to make the communication work. So I said nothing about
the Firebird. She doesn't know." He paused, put one of the
masks under his arm and slipped the freed hand into his
pocket. His thick voice was grim.

"Where is it, Sawyer?" he asked. "What did you do with
the Firebird?"

Rapidly Sawyer cast back over the immediate past. Whenever he had spoken aloud, so that Alper heard him, he had
been denying he had the thing.

"I didn't do anything with it," he said. "I left it where it
was."

The slightest possible tremor shivered through his skull
from the transceiver. Sawyer felt a sudden blaze of murderous
rage ignite in him. He spun toward Alper, making no effort
to control the fury, letting it show in his voice and his face.

"*Stop that!*" he commanded. "You know you can't force
me that way! Once more and I'll make you kill me!"

The tremor ceased. Alper said, "All right, all right. Just
a reminder. I know you aren't lying. I know Nethe searched
you once for the Firebird. I know all she told you, and it
gave me some interesting ideas. I even traced you here by the
transceiver. The strength of the signals was an accurate
guide, once I'd escaped from the Goddess. This attack from
the savages is going to be very useful to all of us. I got free,
Klai got at least a reprive from capture, and you and I are
going to the Temple right away, if the old man will guide us."

He turned toward Zatri, started to speak, then shrugged
and held out one of the masks. Zatri took it gingerly, looking
at Alper with a searching gaze. Alper dipped his head a
little and clapped the pale, smiling thing over his face. He
spoke in a slightly muffled voice.

"I have a plan," he said, "to save your granddaughter. And
incidentally myself, of course. I need your help—"

Zatri held up a hand for patience, hesitated an instant

longer, and then fitted his own mask over his face. It was curious to see the two blank, Isier-featured faces confronting each other, Zatri's blue eyes and Alper's small, cold grey ones blinking through the great ovals of the masks.

Alper repeated his proposal, in English. And Zatri, after an odd moment of complete immobility, as if the result of the mask-donning had startled him, appeared to answer in his own language, quite as if Alper's words had made sense to him. The listening Khom glanced quickly from one to another and began to exchange uneasy murmurs.

"What's happening?" Sawyer asked Klai.

She gave him a wondering look. "The masks are for communication," she said. "Among other things I think Nethe learned English through the use of hers. The Isier, among themselves, have some amazing arts and sciences, so abstract it got to be a problem for a musician, say, to communicate his ideas to a chemist or a physicist. Remember, they've lived for a thousand years, and they've pursued their arts to tremendous heights. They developed this way of exchanging ideas without the need for learning one another's abstract terms. I wonder how Alper managed to steal them."

"So do I," Sawyer said thoughtfully. "I don't trust Alper very far. Listen—what's your grandfather saying?"

"He wants to know Alper's plan. He says he *could* guide him into the Temple—at any other time. Not now. The Ceremony of the Unsealing may have started already. And the streets aren't safe any more."

"I'll tell you exactly what I plan," Alper said, muffled inside the mask. Its thin, pale smile gave him an unfortunate look of conspiratorial malice that might or might not be just. "Sawyer knows where the Firebird is. I must have it! Once I get it, I can force Nethe to open the door back to Earth—"

"How can you force her?" Sawyer asked. The mask swung toward him, smiling. Alper's impatient voice was incongruous behind it.

"You give me the Firebird," he said, "and I'll release you from the transceiver. There, isn't that fair enough? I'll get to Nethe and put it on her. After that she'll do as I tell her."

Sawyer had his private doubts about this, but he did

not voice them, for Zatri was demanding explanations. Rapidly Alper gave them. Zatri spoke to Klai, who led Sawyer forward so Zatri could examine the transceiver clamped to the crown of his skull. But when Sawyer tried to speak, Alper brushed him aside impatiently:

"Don't waste time now. Will you or won't you? You want to get rid of the transceiver. I'll take the Firebird back to Earth with us, and after that I won't need to make trouble at Fortuna. Klai can come too, if she wants. All we have to do is get the Firebird and get to Nethe with the transceiver. She opens the door for the four of us and we go through with the Firebird. All we have to worry about is getting to her before the Ceremony starts."

Zatri asked a question. Klai did not translate, but Alper shrugged and said, "You can't. You'll have to trust me. I—here, wait!"

He pulled the mask from his face and thrust it at Sawyer.

"You put it on. He trusts you. Persuade him, Sawyer. What if the Temple *is* dangerous? Is it any safer here? Tell him he's got to get us to Nethe."

Sawyer looked dubiously at the mask.

"The last time I wore something you gave me, I got the transceiver," he said. "Somehow I don't like the idea of putting this thing over my face. It might turn me into a horned toad, for all I know."

Alper snorted with impatience. "It's perfectly safe. I wore it, didn't I? It's a communication prosthesis. You'll see—the masks convey *form*, the way I've figured it, plus impinging form to give it meaning. Between the Isier it's practically telepathy, but between you and the Khom, there wouldn't be enough memories in common. The masks convey a series of impressions. The human mind's built like a telegraph type of repeater; it triggers kappa wave relays that create new, sharpened, screened impressions. The brain's alpha rhythm may be the carrier wave, using its sweep like a scanning process. I don't know—I'm guessing. But communication's a cortical process, like sight, dependent on form perception, and if necessary an interpreter, like these masks. Language isn't the only form of communication, you know. What about animal communication by scent, a chemical sense? The atomic structure of a chemical scent can be rearranged very easily into a hormone structure, which is simply another language of communication within the body itself. You see?"

"No." Sawyer grinned suddenly. "That's why I'm convinced, maybe."

He ducked his head and fitted the mask over his face. It was smooth and cool, and it clung firmly once he had got it seated well back over his ears. He opened his eyes, looked out through the oval holes. . . .

And instantly something very strange happened. The stable around him leaped into sharp, glorious vividness. He had not seen such clear colors since he was a child. And odors—the smell of hay was a pungent ecstasy, the oil of the swinging lamp sweeter than any incense he had ever smelled. He felt an extraordinary sense of rightness, of location and position—super-orientation, so to speak. Wave motions? The mask must be a booster too, then, a transformer, heightening the impressions it conveyed to the wearer. Naturally, he thought. The faint kappa waves of the brain, the wave-motions of thought, far beyond sensory perception, would have to be transformed to a higher voltage. No wonder Zatri had started and gone rigid when he put on the mask!

And no wonder the Isier thought themselves gods!

He saw Zatri's keen blue eyes looking at him through the opposite mask, out of the white, smirking Isier face.

"Do you understand me?" he asked the old man.

Zatri spoke through his mask. The words were Khom. But what Sawyer heard, felt, sensed was quite different. It was like perceiving an instantaneous building up of shades and patterns, light and sound and meaning, form and scent, indescribable things gradually fading off into peripheral distances where—snap—a gap was leaped, a familiar form took shape in emptiness, and gradually clarified, defined, became more understandable as the semantic periphery of form shaped into—communication. Not gradually. Zatri's echoed words still hung on the air; he had said in perfectly understandable Khom:

"Klai has told me about this man Alper. Do *you* trust him?"

"Certainly not," Sawyer said. "The question is, how much choice do we have?" He nodded toward the noise of howling outside. "It isn't safe anywhere. If the Isier don't break in on us and arrest Klai, the Sselli may break in and kill us all. You have no weapons against them? No explosives, for instance?" He wondered how clearly the words got through to Zatri, how the mask was translating them into the thought-images of the Khom.

"We have a few hoarded explosives," Zatri said. "Illegal, of course. What they would do against the Sselli I don't know. But can you imagine the Isier letting any weapons exist that would harm the Sselli, when they are equally vulnerable? There *is* one weapon the Isier could use, however, and I think they'll have to, very soon. But it means danger to the Isier too, so naturally they hesitate. They—"

He broke off at the sound of tapping on the door. A Khom put his head in, murmured something and withdrew. Zatri glanced away and then back to Sawyer.

"The Temple towers are beginning to glow," he said. "That means the Ceremony is starting. It must mean Nethe has already entered the Hall of the Worlds and will never come out again—as Nethe. The Goddess will kill her or die. If Nethe wins, the Mask and Robe will be sealed on her, and she'll be the Goddess herself. So you see your friend's plan is useless. Only as a sacrifice could a human being enter the Hall of the Worlds now."

He glanced uneasily at Klai. Sawyer glanced too, and was half stunned by the incredible loveliness the mask lent her pretty face. He looked at Alper, and was relieved to notice that the old man's beauty was not noticeably enhanced. He relayed what Zatri had just said. Alper snorted impatiently.

"Nethe needs the Firebird," he said. "There must be some way to get within sight of her and hold it up where she can see it. Once that happens, I guarantee she'll break up *any* ceremony and jump for the Firebird. Without it she's bound to lose the contest with the Goddess. Just get me to Nethe, *with* the Firebird. She'll do as she's told. She'll open the Gateway and we'll all go through, back to Earth."

Klai had been translating this in a murmur to her grandfather, he eyes watchful on Alper's face. Zatri said irresolutely, "The Gateway you speak of is too dangerous. Too uncertain. I don't—"

"Klai went through it, didn't she?" Alper demanded angrily when this was translated to him.

Zatri said, speaking to Sawyer, "I sent Klai after Nethe through the Gateway. It was a terribly dangerous thing, but the only way I knew. I hid her deep down underground, waiting for Nethe to come to a place where I knew she went sometimes to work her—magic."

"And what happened?" Sawyer asked.

"I wish I knew. I've watched Nethe many times when she didn't know. I've seen her make fire spring out between her fingers and open a—a whirling spiral in the air. I didn't know about the Firebird then. But I knew she went through the spiral and out of the world. Sometimes she was gone a long time. I thought there might be hope for Klai elsewhere, for I knew there was none here."

"I remember—a little," Klai put in. "I remember Grandfather pushing me through, and how fast Nethe went, and how I fell on the ground in a strange, dark place. Then Nethe made fire spring out again in her fingers—that was the Firebird, I know now—and another spiral opened, and—" She shook her head. "I woke in the uranium mine, not knowing anything except my own name."

She had spoken in English, and Alper said quickly, "I've got a hunch that the dark place you mention was the Under-Shell. The Goddess told me a good deal, you know. She was desperate to find out all she could about Nethe, and I pumped her. I think the Gateway's a circular process, which may—"

"How about the Goddess?" Sawyer asked. "If she's that desperate, couldn't we do business with her, somehow?"

"No. Why should she bother? I sounded her out on that, and I know. Remember, to the Isier we're so many uninteresting animals. They're immortals. But the Firebird is the—the keystone of their immortality. Don't you know what it must be, Sawyer? I'll give you a hint. You can buy variations of the Firebird for three for a dime, back on Earth. But—not *the* Firebird."

He drew a long breath.

"The Well of the Worlds is miraculous enough," he said, "and I have no idea how that works, though I've guessed a little. It's a link between Khom'ad and Earth now, bonding the two worlds together—but it was also the channel through which the Isier got their energy from other dimensions, other continua. It's a—a tube that must be made of a form of matter that isn't really matter at all. Unstable, dynamic matter. Here at this end, in Khom'ad, it's Khom'ad matter, but the other end of the Well—that's Earth-matter, right now. The other end of the Well can flux into whatever type of matter it touches in the non-Khom'ad plenum. It must be simply an absolutely adaptable form of matter, capable of instant adaptation to whatever type of matter exists in whatever other-space Khom'ad drifts through. How else could the contact be made at all and the channel for the energy maintained? That's half of it, Sawyer—only half, the material half, the oil-bath in an ordinary fluid clutch. But the other half is the matrix of magnetic particles that saturates the oil, the vital other half that makes a fluid clutch work.

"The Well of the Worlds is a perfectly adaptable type of matter. But the Firebird is simply this.

"It is the perfect conductor.

"It must be. What else fits? It gave me energy—life—and that energy had to come from somewhere. And it could have come from anywhere at all, from space itself, from the uranium in the mine, from—anything. What the Firebird does is form perfect conductivity between whatever it touches and whatever energy-source is nearest. That's how it opens the Gateways between worlds, I suppose. Conductivity—matter to energy—how can I tell? Perhaps it acts as conductor, under certain circumstances, to the wave-motions of Khom'ad when you're on Earth, so that your physical body—made up of wave-motions—is altered to the Khom'ad wave-motion, and we see that alteration as a Gateway, whereas the metamorphosis is simply in *us*.

"Perhaps that's why only an Isier can open the Gateway. The Isier aren't entirely matter, as we know it, any more than the Well is. Didn't Nethe say they'd made themselves into isotopes? What they did, of course, was to alter the wave-motion of their physical bodies, so that they changed into a form of matter which could receive energy directly from the Well, as the new dry batteries can use oxygen from the air instead of depending on their own chemicals."

Alper smiled a little. "Back on Earth, every house wired for electricity uses something like the Firebird. Remember, the Firebird's built to open and close. It's a safety fuse, Sawyer. A perfect conductor that's also a safety fuse. That's why it was able to shut itself off when Khom'ad drifted in contact with the Earth and the uranium mine. The other end of the Well adapted to Earth-matter, and all the tremendous energies of the uranium would have come pouring through into Khom'ad if the Well had been able to conduct it. But when the Firebird closed, the Well became inert, as far as energy-conductivity went. The physical bond between Khom'ad and Earth still exists, but that's all. I suppose that's why the Firebirds don't appear in Khom'ad, though they're glimpsed down in the Well sometimes. If they're energy-forms, how can they pass through a non-conductor?

"But if the Firebird is dropped open into the Well, I don't know what might happen. It's a safety fuse, but there's such a thing as a proximity fuse too. And there are perfectly unimaginable energy-sources all around us now, and perhaps only non-conductivity saves us from—I don't know what. Even the Isier might be vulnerable to perfect conductivity, if enough energy poured into them. Now they get only the energy they gain from the sacrifices that go down the Well of the Worlds. And it isn't enough.

"For they disappear, whenever they've discharged enough energy. Where do they go? Somehow, somewhere, they regain their lost energy and return, through the ice-hall. Suppose they gained more energy than they could hold? The Goddess is afraid of something, Sawyer. I think there's a safety factor involved, just as the Firebird's ability to shut itself off is a safety factor. The Isier may be isotopes of matter, but remember it isn't a form of matter we know anything about—matter like the Well, for all I know. How can I tell what kind of unknown safety factor might have come into action when the Isier first turned themselves into gods? There must have been one, and when the Firebird was stolen perhaps a different one became necessary. I don't know what. But I do know the Goddess and Nethe are both afraid of something, and that's why, if Zatri will only co-operate, we can all get away safe. You tell him that, Sawyer!"

Klai had again been translating the essentials in a quick murmur as Alper spoke. Now Zatri looked at Sawyer with a steady gaze through the eye-holes of the mask.

"Ask this man," he said, "why he does all this."

"To get the Firebird, of course," Alper said impatiently when this was passed on to him. "I want to get to Earth with the Firebird. What more do I need?"

"And what will the Firebird give him?" Zatri asked.

"Immortality," Alper answered after a pause. He shook his ponderous head. "What else would I want? Youth, strength, immortality. Isn't it enough?" Klai translated.

Zatri said in a quiet voice, "Why should I loose on your world, your Earth, a new immortal who might begin another Isier race? Your people are like mine. Human, not gods. No, there must be no more immortals! I am an old man too. Tell Alper this—that I know it is right to grow old. To see death coming as a welcome rest. No man who strives like a child after eternal youth is fit for immortality. Oh, no! I'll not see this Earthman gain the Firebird and grow immortal! I will not guide him to the Temple!"

Sawyer laughed in sudden, relieved delight. "Good for you, Zatri!" he said. "I don't trust him either! And he can kill me with the transceiver if he wants to—" Here he swung around toward Alper and stared defiantly at him through the mask "—but I won't help you either! If you want the Firebird, you'll have to take my orders, not—"

Alper swung his arm up with violent impatience.

"That's enough!" he said. "I expected it. Now take the consequences, and remember, you asked for it!"

While they all stared, Alper lifted his heavy voice and shouted. From just outside the door the deep, belling Isier voices answered. Before anyone in the startled group could stir, the door crashed open, torn from its hinges by the casual sweep of an Isier arm, and in the opening two tremendous robed gods stood, with a third looming behind them, looking in casual contempt at the stable and all inside it.

With one quick snatch Alper tore the mask from Sawyer's

face. The world went back to normal color and scent and sound. It was like a film, Sawyer thought, changing from technicolor to drab black and white. He jumped just too late to get the mask back. Alper clapped it over his face and spoke through it, muffled but distinct. And it seemed that the Isier understood, though their own masks clung to the backs of their godlike heads, not the faces.

"You can arrest the girl," Alper said calmly. "The Goddess wants her for the sacrifice. This man here and the old man come with us. The rest you can exterminate." He turned to Sawyer, his eyes gleaming in cold triumph through the smirking mask.

"Now," he said. "This is your last chance, my boy. I want the Firebird!"

XI

Sawyer's mind was clicking rapidly, alertly, and so far perfectly futilely. A dozen useless ideas flickered through it as Alper's demand still hung upon the breathless silence of the stable. From outside the deep booming of a Sselli charge made the walls shake. Humans shouted and there was the heavy, shuddering trample and thump of struggling bodies perilously close outside.

"Quick!" Alper said, slipping his hand toward his pocket. "I hold every card, Sawyer! Don't be a fool. I can kill you. I can knock you senseless. The Isier can tear you apart. Give me the Firebird and you have everything to win. Refuse, and—"

One of the Isier let out a deep, resonant sigh of impatience and moved forward like a marble angel walking, lifting his great robed arm. He said something in his own language, serene contempt on his face. He stepped around Sawyer, seized Klai by the arm with one tremendous hand and sent her spinning across the stable toward the two gods in the door. They opened to let her pass, and the farther Isier swept her up under his arm and turned away into the darkness.

Sawyer's futile, unthinking leap after her was halted

sharply by the grip of marble the nearer Isier locked about his shoulder. His teeth rattled as the tall god shook him.

"Wait!" Alper shouted. "Isier, wait! Let me handle this. The Goddess bargained with me, remember!"

The Isier sighed again, but let Sawyer regain his footing.

"Sawyer, let's be sensible," Alper said impatiently. "Look, now. I did bargain—"

He stopped abruptly, with a glance at the nearest Isier, and then raised his hands to tilt the mask up and away from his face. "I don't want them to understand what I'm saying—because I told the Goddess I'd get the Firebird for her. Shes' got to have it back, and she's got to keep its theft a secret. I think Nethe took it, not the Goddess. But the main thing is that it's gone and the Goddess would promise anything to get it back. If I don't bring it, she'll kill me. And my life's important to you, remember. I die—you die. What do you say, Sawyer?"

Sawyer listened to the noise of the fight, so near outside now they had to pitch their voices loud to sound above it. He knew he would have to act fast. The next step would almost certainly be an order from Alper to have him searched, on the off-chance that the Firebird had found its way back into his pocket since Nethe's search, some hours ago. He had to forestall that, and there was no time to waste. He shot one glance at the alert Zatri, still wearing his mask.

"All right," Sawyer said. "You win." He moved his shoulder a little, feeling the warm spot that was the hidden Firebird shift against his side. He said, "It isn't on me, but I'll get it. I'll need a light. Hold everything."

"Don't show it," Alper said quickly. "The Isier mustn't see—"

At Sawyer's nod Alper sighed and let go of the tilted mask, so that it dropped back and covered his face again. Sawyer took three steps forward and reached up for the swinging lantern. Every eye was riveted on him, every face tense with expectation. Zatri's blue eyes blazed through the mask. No one knew what to expect next, but the Khom looked ready for anything.

Sawyer laughed aloud in one reckless burst of grim amusement. With a single strong pitch he sent the lantern straight into the haymow at his shoulder. The Khom who crowded it leaped both ways to give it room, and from a corner of his eye Sawyer was gratified to see someone kick hay helpfully over the flame as he jumped. They could have no idea what he planned, but this much was evident—he wanted a fire.

In the same motion that sent the lantern flying, Sawyer hurtled forward upon Alper, the hand that released the lantern clamping instantly on Alper's wrist. He snapped the man toward him, locked his other wrist in a bone-breaking grip, and shouted, "Zatri!"

There was no need to shout. Zatri was off the bale and yelling crisp orders before the lantern had more than struck the hay. There was a moment of wildest confusion, in which the two tall Isier, roaring together on a single note of outrage and surprise, surged forward toward the struggling pair. But in a low, dark wave between them the Khom rose up from the floor in one simultaneous surge, hurling themselves doggedly upon the towering gods.

The Isier staggered at the unexpected impact. Then they planted their feet wide and struck angrily at the swarming pack. Every blow that landed snapped bone. And there was no way in which a Khom could hurt a god. But they could hamper them. And desperation made them reckless.

Sawyer needed every ounce of strength in him to control the great bulk and the ponderous weight of the man he held. For the first few moments he thought he was going to fail, and then, quite suddenly, Alper gave up.

Sawyer thought it was a trick, and held his grip desperately. Then he realized the truth. Alper's first try had been the only try he could afford. He had strength—but limited strength. After he exhausted the Firebird power he would relapse into senile helplessness. He dared not struggle. He would conserve his little store of energy, and wait. Sawyer twisted the old man's arms behind him and paused, panting, to survey the scene of conflict.

Smoke already veiled it. The fire had caught and was crackling up in the oil-soaked hay with a roar that grew to a deafening burst of sound in a matter of seconds. The stable filled with blinding light and scorching heat, driving Isier and Khom alike toward the broken door.

106

The ponies, whinnying in shrill terror, were plunging over the low barrier of their stalls. There was total confusion as the whole swaying, kicking, roaring melee surged outward through the door and into the alley, Sawyer and Alper borne willy-nilly with them out of the burning stable.

From the street at the alley's end sounded the deep-toned booming of a savage, very near and drawing nearer. The fire had served its purpose. Sawyer had never hoped the Khom could control two Isier, no matter how they outnumbered them, but he thought the savages could, if the fire flared up in time.

He set his teeth and without warning chopped Alper across the temple. Alper grunted and went down.

"Zatri!" Sawyer shouted at the top of his voice, looking wildly around. The old man was hanging stubbornly on an Isier wrist, his arms wrapping the long, ice-robed arm. Above him the serene face bent, sweat beading it but no emotion showing on the cold, smiling features. The Isier shook his other arm free of the crowd that pressed him in and lifted a great white fist over Zatri's head. Sawyer yelled a futile warning. The fist was already sweeping down, and Zatri's moments seemed numbered.

Then, without the slightest warning, the Isier vanished.

Blinding light and bursting heat marked the space in empty air where he had stood. For an instant a cloud of dispersing molecules seemed to hang upon the air. Energy had failed him, and he had whirled helplessly away upon whatever mysterious, vanishing cycle the Isier traveled when the soundless summons called them.

Zatri staggered back, shaking his scorched head with the mask still miraculously clinging to it, so that a dwarfed Isier with white ruffled hair seemed to be still ludicrously clasping a vanished arm.

Sawyer reached down and pulled the mask from Alper's face. It came unwillingly, clasping the head with a firmness that showed why even the exertion of fighting had not unseated it. Sawyer pressed it over his own face with one hand, seeing the world come suddenly back to technicolor vividness.

Alper was suddenly conscious again, his eyes glaring up at them. His hand went toward his pocket. Sawyer bent, trapped the hand, hove the big man roughly to his feet.

"This way," Zatri said, breathless but calm. "Come along!" and they set off down the alley toward its blind end, squeezing past the blaze of the stable. Alper was a ponderous weight between them.

A door at the alley's end gave under Zatri's expert attention. He shouted across his shoulder to his men, and Sawyer, looking back, saw the single remaining Isier locked in a Laocoon struggle with a dozen sinuous, writhing Sselli, their eyes blazing golden in the reflected firelight.

This was the moment for which Alper must have been hoarding all his remaining strength. For with one enormous, desperate heave he threw all his great bulk into the balance and snapped the hold Sawyer and Zatri had locked upon his arms. He reeled back against the firelit wall, gasping, laughing, triumphant, his hand dropping like a striking snake toward his pocket.

Sawyer, staggering from that mighty thrust which must have used up a dangerous supply of energy, braced himself for the killing shock. But Alper, hand upon the control, could afford to speak first. He jerked his big head toward Zatri and said, still gasping for breath:

"Tell him—got to lead us—to the Temple, now!"

"Whose side are you on, Alper?" Sawyer asked wearily. "Was all that planning back there a trick? Or were you lying when you said the Goddess made a bargain?"

"I'm on Alper's side, you young fool," Alper assured him, still half-drunk with his sudden victory. "No, it wasn't a trick. Or a lie. She did bargain—my life for the Firebird. But I don't believe her. I told you, we're lower than dogs to the Isier. She might spare my life but she wouldn't send me home and she certainly wouldn't give me the Firebird. I want that or nothing. That's why my plan about Nethe still stands—if the old man will lead us. Will he?" He moved his hand in his pocket significantly. "You'd better talk him into it, my boy!"

The words could have meant nothing to Zatri, but the motion did, and Zatri had his own ideas about the immediate future. In the wavering firelight he seemed to flicker with

108

swift action as his hand shot out, casting a loop of silvery cord. . . .

The coil of it flashed downward about Alper's neck and drew tight, tight, cut into the jowled throat stanglingly. Alper stood perfectly motionless. But he spoke.

"Tell him to drop it," he said. "Sawyer! It's your life!"

"Say no," Zatri told Sawyer quietly. "I can guess what he said. I'm sorry, young man, but I must think of Klai now. Tell him not to move until I order it. I can kill him with one pull. I am old, but I'm strong."

"Sawyer, do you want to die?" Alper demanded desperately. "Tell him—"

"He says of course you can kill me," Sawyer said, almost with indifference. "But you'll die first. He's thinking of Klai, Alper. I don't—"

Zatri said, "Tell him he must take his hand from his pocket. Tell him I'll pull the noose if he doesn't. He fears death—he'll do as I say. I think he knows that no life, not yours or my own, can stand between me and what I must do now."

Sawyer translated. Slowly, sullenly, Alper lifted his hand from his pocket. Sawyer had a sudden spark of hope and said, "Zatri, make him release me from the transceiver!"

Alper burst out violently, "No! I won't do that! As long as I have that I've got—even if you kill me—no!—"

"He would not," Zatri said. "I know. We're both old men, Alper and I, and we understand each other." He chuckled softly. "I'll lead you to the Temple now. Do you know why I changed my mind, why I'll give Alper his chance at the Firebird and immortality?"

"Why?" Sawyer asked.

"It takes more than the Firebird to make a man a god," Zatri said. "I'm too old—my mind wasn't clear about this until just now. Alper could achieve immortality, yes—but never invulnerability!" He smiled. "Tell him that," he said.

Zatri said softly through the mask, "Beyond this point, we talk in whispers."

Sawyer looked back along the low tunnel twisting out of sight. They had come a long and devious way underground since they left the noisy streets. Zatri, still carefully holding the cord that noosed Alper's neck, was fumbling at the wall. Rectangular stone blocks hewn perhaps a thousand years ago had been put together with a luminous mortar that glowed with a clear, soft light, so that they stood in what looked like an endless trellis of shining squares.

Zatri gave a little sigh of satisfaction and a door-sized square of the wall before him went dead, the glowing mortar fading as if a switch had cut off a flow of electrons through it. He pushed gently and the whole square receded, letting a soft golden light shine into the trellised passage.

"If we're lucky," Zatri said, turning his masked face to Sawyer, "there won't be any guards outside. The ceremony's under way, and all the Isier who aren't out fighting should be in the Hall of the Worlds. We're directly under it now, and the cells of the sacrifices are just outside. There's no danger of their escaping." He chuckled with a curious, sardonic note Sawyer did not understand. "The only way they could escape," he said, "is a way the Isier needn't worry about. Come along, and be careful!"

Sawyer followed the two old men through the wall.

It seemed to him that he had stepped out at the foot of Niagara. He stood half-stunned for a moment, his head craned back, staring up at the golden waterfall which rose up, up, up into misty infinities overhead. They stood at the foot of a long ramp that wound upward across the face of the waterfall in gentle zig-zags like a streak of frozen lightning patterning the golden sway above.

The sway was the motion of curtains that looked as if they were woven of bright gold light, hanging straight out of a golden sky. Tier after tier of them rippled slowly in deep, changing folds to no tangible breeze, brushing the ramp with level after ascending level of golden hems.

"We go up," Zatri said in a whisper. "Keep still, both of you. If anyone comes, get behind the curtains—and pray!"

They went fast, stilling the noise of their feet on the ramps. At the third level Zatri began to twitch the curtains aside and peer quickly behind them without pausing in his climb. At the fifth level they found her. . . .

A tiny room like a bee's cell opened behind its curtain,

hexagonal, walled with a continual crawl of colors that flowed, merged, faded and renewed themselves continually in a motion so compelling the eye followed them in fascinated wonder.

"Don't look," Zatri warned them. "That's hypnosis. Tell Alper. We need him."

Sawyer murmured his warning without turning his head, for he was staring through the blurred wall at the dreaming figure of Klai, kneeling upon the small hexagon of the cell's floor, her hands loose in her lap, her head thrown back, staring up in a daze at the changing spectra as they crept across the walls.

Through the blur of colors, Sawyer caught a glimpse of a chamber beyond so vast, so overpoweringly strange that he jerked his gaze away instinctively, afraid to look, afraid to believe his eyes.

Zatri rapped softly on the glassy wall of the hexagon before him. Klai stirred a little, a very little, and subsided again, her head lolling back, her eyes upon the patterns. He rapped again. Very slowly she turned.

"Good," Zatri said in a whisper. "It's not too late. We can still save her. Young man—" He turned, fixing Sawyer with a strangely intent gaze. "I have something to ask you," he said softly. "Listen carefully. I have my own plan all laid. It involves risk to everyone. I want you to understand that can't be helped. There's no alternative for any of us except a life of endless slavery under the Isier rule."

He paused, gave Sawyer a look of curious appeal, and said, "So I must ask you this. *Do you have the Firebird now?*"

Sawyer hesitated, trying to read the meaning behind the old man's intent blue gaze. He could not. But after a long moment of uncertainty, he said:

"Yes. I do."

Zatri let out a deep sigh. "I'm glad," he said. "It may mean we all live in spite of everything."

Alper had been watching this exchange with a restless gaze full of suspicion. "What's he saying?" he demanded of Sawyer. "Translate!"

"Be still!" Zatri twitched the cord slightly, then made a quick gesture urging patience. "One more thing before we

111

act," he told Sawyer. "You see Klai in there, helpless, hypno-tized. There's one way of releasing her, and one way only." He laughed softly. "The Isier know us very well. They can leave the cells unguarded, because no one can release a prisoner—*without taking the prisoner's place.*"

As he spoke, he moved. And he moved with that startling speed he could call upon when he had to, old as he was. Sawyer went staggering against the cell-wall at the unes-pected hard push the old man gave him. He struck it with one shoulder, staggered and felt the wall give beneath his weight—

XII

THERE WAS a moment of total disorientation. The cell walls seemed to fold inward upon themselves in a complex, precise motion like a well-organized machine. As he struck the floor inside the cell he saw Klai swept helplessly outward by the same action that had carried him in. The cell was a relentless trap. As he struggled to his feet on the hexagonal flooring, thrusting hard against the wall in a vain attempt to turn it again, he saw Zatri's masked face pressed close to the crawl of the spectrum in the glass, heard the old man's voice speaking softly and clearly.

"I'm sorry, young man," Zatri said. "I came here to take that place myself. But I think this is a better way than if I were there, because with you inside, it need not be a way that ends in death. For you, there's a chance. For anyone else—" He made a gesture of finality.

Klai had fallen to her knees on the ramp beside Zatri. Gently he went to lift her. Sawyer watched them through a crawl of colors so hypnotic he could not focus on them without feeling sleep cloud his brain. He rapped on the glass.

"Quick!" he said. "I—I'm dizzy. If you have anything to say, say it! Or is this outright murder?"

"Shut your eyes!" Zatri said. "Don't look at the colors while I talk. No, it isn't murder—or if it is, we all die anyhow, and you'll have had your chance to save yourself and the rest of us with you. Maybe the whole race. I'm not forcing

112

you into anything I wouldn't do myself, if I could. But only you wear the—the amulet, the transceiver. So that only you can resist the hypnosis, when the crisis of the ceremony comes. *Only you.*" He glanced at Alper, watching all this with impatient eyes. He twitched the cord ever so slightly.

"As he holds your life, I hold his," he said. "And I value no life, not even my own, above the goal I'm seeking. If Alper would release you and put the device on me, I'd change places with you. But he wouldn't. So you must go into the ceremony as a sacrifice—but not unarmed. You have the transceiver. You carry the Firebird. You have a chance no other man could hope for.

"This is *my* goal. To break the Isier rule and free my people. I know it isn't yours, but I can't spare myself or you. I *must* do what I can to achieve that purpose. Now listen, because there isn't much time. At any moment you may be swept into the ceremony."

Sawyer, listening tensely, his eyes closed, heard Klai begin to murmur something in a voice of drowsy alarm and opened his eyes long enough to see, through the crawl of colors, the girl lifting her head and staring around dazedly. Zatri hushed her with a gentle shake of the shoulder.

"You'll go into the ceremony," he went on. "But not helpless. Not hypnotized into blind obedience. Because when you feel yourself slipping, you must call on Alper to touch the control of the transceiver, gently, very gently, I'll make sure of that. He explained enough of it so that I feel sure the lightest shaking of sound in your head will be enough to break the hypnosis.

"What happens in the ceremony no one knows exactly. But it is known that the victims must be hypnotized before the Firebirds can feed. Before your time comes, my Khom may be able to save you. I told you we have explosives. I hope to destroy enough of the Temple to let the Sselli in. That's our plan. If it works in time, you'll be safe.

"The Temple towers will be a blaze of light before tonight's ceremony ends, and the Sselli will be flocking around the walls, battering to get in. If we're lucky we'll breach the walls of the Hall of the Worlds itself, and turn the Sselli in upon the Isier.

"Then there'll be fighting!" The old man's eyes glowed behind the mask. "Then the Isier will have to unleash their last weapons. It's our hope the Sselli will succeed in turning them against the Isier. But if the Sselli fail, there's one chance left. It all depends on you." He hesitated.

"Do you hear me?" he asked. "Open your eyes for a moment. I want to be sure. Yes, yes. Then listen—if you see the Isier winning, judge your time. When it seems right to you—somehow you must reach the Well. Somehow you must drop the Firebird down—and drop it *open*."

Sawyer for the first time was moved to speech.

"But—Alper said—"

"Alper was right. It means danger. But the immortality of the Isier depends on the Well. We can't kill them. But—think we can kill the Well itself. True, that may also wipe out the whole city. It may send the Upper Shell crashing through to the Under-Shell. But—" Zatri chuckled grimly. "If the Isier win, you die! Would you rather die a victim, or a conqueror? Alone, or with a race of gods to go with you? And knowing that what men remain alive afterward will owe their freedom and their future to what you did?"

Zatri was silent after that, breathing rather hard through his mask. Presently he said, "There isn't much time. You'd better tell Alper as much as you think suitable. It might be better not to mention the final plan, if everything else fails —about the Firebird, I mean. If he realizes it's lost to him, he may not cooperate." He coughed gently.

"Look at me, young man," he said. "Just for a second. I don't ask your forgiveness, but I want to say again I'm doing this because I must. If you die, we all die. If you win, we win with you. I wish I could do the job myself. Do you believe me?"

Sawyer met his eyes through the coiling spectra in the glass.

"I believe you. I don't mention forgiveness. If I come out of this alive, you'll answer for what you've done. But I believe you." He turned his head. "Alper, I—" He stared. "Alper! Zatri, wake him up!"

The big old man was lolling half helpless against the glass at Zatri's side, peering through the cell walls with their

114

irresistible hypnosis of motion and color. Zatri jumped to shake him awake. Klai watched them with drowsy wonder. Sawyer kept calling, over and over, as loudly as he dared, "Alper! Alper, do you hear me! Alper, wake up!"

"I'm awake," the big man snarled abruptly fighting Zatri off. "I'm all right. But—Sawyer! Have you looked! Do you realize what they've got in there?"

Sawyer had not looked. After his first glimpse of infinite, whirling space beyond the wall of cells, and the lashing, twining coils of fire that spun in it, he had had no attention to spare.

"You've got to listen," he said. "If you want the Firebird, you've got to. Alper, do you hear me?"

"Yes, yes," Alper said, his attention only half fixed. "What's the matter?"

Sawyer told him, speaking fast and glossing over the question of the Firebird as well as he could. But Alper was muttering to himself.

"The heart of the atom," he was saying. "The atomic dance! Electrons in—yes, seven shells! And the—the fire circles *inside* the chamber they're weaving. Sawyer, do you realize what they've got in there? I half guessed it before, but it took this to make me realize—"

Sawyer blinked and looked at Alper through an incomprehensible blurring haze he could not understand. What was wrong? His own eyes? The cell walls had begun to shimmer a little. Alper's voice came through it shaken too, as if both sound and light waves vibrated in tune with the shaking walls.

"It's a cyclotron!" Alper said. "A cosmotron, a synchrotron, whatever you like. Something inside there is serving as an oscillator to drive forces around and around the chamber the electrons make. A planetary cyclotron! Somewhere there must be a focusing aperture to release the pencil of high-energy rays, because—you see the green beams? Sawyer, do you see?"

The voice blurred, the face with it, Zatri's anxious eyes peering through the smiling Isier mask, Klai's slowly wakening figure behind them. Pure vibration made every molecule of his body shiver in unison with the shivering walls. The

115

colors were moving inward from the walls toward the center of his brain, and with the last despairing flicker of awareness he called to Alper for help. . . .

The smallest of sounds whispered delicately through the chambers of Sawyer's brain. The whisper grew louder. The blood-beat began to roar like a far-away lion. . . .

Sawyer struggled up to the surface of consciousness and called into the golden blur that hemmed him in, "That's enough. Alper, that's enough!" Miraculously, at that, the roar began swiftly to fade until it was only a whisper again of breath rustling through chambers of bone and blood beating deep and full in the arteries that keep the mind alive.

The cell walls no longer surrounded him. He was closed inside a shell of light and he knew the shell was the turning walls of the hexagon, though he himself felt no sensation of turning. He was the hub. The walls pivoted upon him. And the blur of their turning was a thousand times more hypnotic than the blur of colors had been. His mind tugged eagerly to spin with them, into the blurring of oblivion. Only that quiver of constant sound kept him in control.

He remembered what Alper had been saying when the cell walls shut out the sight of him. Atoms. The atomic dance, and the whirl of the cyclotron. The cell walls were an electronic shell closing him in, he thought, and he was the nucleus they turned around. He was growing light-headed with motion. . . .

Far away, hanging head downward in a golden sky, a crescent of Isier were sitting on thrones of gold, upside down in the firmament. But Isier reduced to the size of dolls. Vertigo seized Sawyer violently as sight came slowly back to him. The crescent that floated in space expanded and whirled before him until its ends joined in a circle, but a circle so vast his mind could not accept it. This was what he had glimpsed through the cell-wall in the great, whirling void beyond. He tried in vain to coerce his mind back to reason. He could only stare.

The ranks of solemn angels were ranged in one tremendous circle, facing inward, supported upon nothing at all. They floated free in swimming golden space, and—no, was that a reflection glimmering here and there around their feet? Was it a flat platform under the thrones, invisible, made of clear glass?

Not all the thrones had angels in them. There were broad gaps, one Isier surrounded by vacant seats, then a group of three or four with emptiness on both sides. Where were the rest? Fighting in the streets? Not all. Not even a majority. Perhaps a third of the circle of thrones were occupied. Then the remainder must be those who had gone into vapor when their energy lapsed, and dispersed them upon that strange cycle which they had to take at a word of command none could understand or deny.

In the center of the ring was a sphere of something so bright Sawyer could not look at it. Two tall figures faced each other across the brightness, and a dazzle of green lightnings flashed between them. But he was moving too fast. He could not focus on this or anything—yet. For he was swinging in a wide, bewildering orbit. Far under him now he could see the glass-crowned heads with their blank, serene, backward-staring masks and their vividly alive, forward-staring faces. Watching the future and the past, he thought.

Now his great orbit swung him past them and down, down, down beyond the level of the thrones, far under, toward a vast bowl of golden haze which seemed to form the undersky of the tremendous hollow sphere he whirled in. Looking up, he could see the golden thrones from below, set solid on square bases, and countless Isier feet planted in pairs, flat upon nothingness.

He swung up again on the far side. The level platform with the thrones was a lenticular nebula which he saw edgewise and then slowly dawning into an elipse ringed all around with double-faced heads, and then broadening into a flat circle again straight down. But he could not look straight down, because of that intolerable glare in the center.

Out of it streamed those lashing coils of fire which he had dimly glimpsed from beyond the cell-wall. They flowed writhing and circling through the void in which he spun, circumscribed by it in a way he had not yet begun to grasp, so that the space inside the globe was filled by their tremendous spiraling.

He was not alone in his flight through golden space and

golden spears of light. Other blurs of brilliance swung in other orbits around the galaxy of the gods. Other kneeling, human figures, motionless inside the spinning shells that carried them upon their orbits around that fiery sun. He could not count them, there were so many. But he remembered what Alper had said, and by craning and shielding his eyes he made out the number of the orbits. Seven. Seven orbits in which countless electrons spun around a nucleus too bright to see.

And it was growing brighter. As he squinted at it through almost closed lids, a kneeling figure enclosed in its spinning shell of force dropped toward the center of the glare, hovered for a second, dark against that light, and then vanished straight into the heart of the fire, between the two Isier who stood facing each other across it. Instantly the fire flared high, in a burst that scorched the eyes.

And between the two figures green lightnings crackled anew.

Sawyer tried hard to make his thoughts fall into a pattern he could grasp. Too much was happening. He could see too much, and none of it understandable. The blur of the spinning walls that carried him on his orbit was still hypnotic, though that steadying noise in his skull helped hold the sleep at bay.

"Give me a little more, Alper," he said, and his voice rebounded fantastically from the whirl of the walls. He thought of the disc in Alper's hand, and his own words whispering out of it, and the image was more disorienting than what he saw around him. "A little, not much. There—there! Good."

The noise was louder. He could think a little better. But what was happening was still so incoherent he groped frantically for analogies to give it pattern.

"I'm the axis the cell turns on," he thought. "I'm the proton that swings the electron of the walls around. But in this vaster space, I'm an electron whirling around the nucleus of the fire down there. Who knows what an electron's made of, anyhow? Nobody." An instantaneous vision of all electrons in the make-up of all matter swam before his eyes, every one of them a miniature Sawyer kneeling in a spinning hex-

118

agon. He shook the picture out of his mind with a tremendous effort.

What was the blinding sphere of light that controlled all these whirling things? The nucleus of this atom with seven shells of force? (A uranium atom? he wondered dimly. Rich and complex with its great cloud of whirling electrons in seven shells around a tight-packed nucleus?) Uranium was the element the Firebirds sucked out of Earth's pole. Then might that sphere of brilliance be—

"The Well!" he thought. *"The Well of the Worlds!"* And he strained his dazzled eyes toward it, trying hard to make out what the thing was, his mind trying in vain to pierce its brilliance and see the far end where the world of Khom'ad lay locked to the world of Earth. . . .

He could not. But he could see more clearly, as his vision adjusted to its limit of tolerance, the two figures facing each other across that blinding blaze. A white-robed figure, and a column of swaying, lashing darkness upon which a pale mask floated.

The Goddess. Nethe and the Goddess.

Then this was the Unsealing, from which one or the other would walk alive, leaving a vanquished rival dead beside the Well. How, he wondered in awed amazement, could the Isier die? In what unimaginable form would death overtake the undying gods?

The rings of electrons spun. The fiery streamers of light poured swirling inside the shell of the electrons. And between the two rival Goddesses the sphere of the Well burned high and then low again, as one victim after another whirled downward toward the flame, hovered, dropped. With each victim, the fire flared high.

"And they're being replaced from outside," Sawyer thought. "As each drops from the middle ring into the fire, a readjustment must take place all through the seven orbits. Cell by cell they snatch us from the wall of sacrifices and whirl us into the dance as they need us. We—"

A sudden jolt knocked the thoughts out of his head. He was dropping nearer the fire . . . The outermost orbit of the seven acquired a new electron and the sixth received Sawyer.

Presently, he thought, the fifth would rob the sixth of him, and so, step by step, he would fall through the dance of the rings until he hovered above the innermost flame, and dropped. . . .

To replenish the weapons with which the Goddess and the Goddess-elect were lashing each other with whips of emerald flame. What were the weapons? How did they draw upon the burning Well for their power?

As if in answer, for a moment the fire died between them and he could look down clearly and see. For one of the falling electrons was hesitating above the Well. Had some helpless sacrifice, for an instant, jolted half-awake as he dropped toward immolation?

The green fires faded, ceased. The Well filmed over for an instant and it was possible for Sawyer to gaze unblinded upon the heart of the ceremony. He could still not bear to look upon the complex pattern that seethed in the Well. But he could see the two Isier, pausing as if for a moment's breath before the combat began again.

Nethe's great, baleful, half-lidded eyes like a snake's eyes —or like a Sselli's—glowed with an inner flame as hot as the Well's. Her face was wet with a luminous dew of sweat, and her robes showed great rents whose edges glowed as if fire had ripped them and ignited an undying line of pale-green ember wherever it touched. She was swaying to and fro as a snake sways, restlessly and endlessly, incapable of standing still because the forces of destruction burned so high in her even while she snatched this moment's rest.

With the same fierce, snake-like motion the Goddess swayed. Her robes of blackness the color of oblivion were rent too, and glowing with pale-green embers along every slash.

Something was wrong about their heads. And he could not quite make out the strangely shaped weapons they held shoulder-high between their hands as they faced each other.

Then with a shock he realized what had happened. They had removed their masks. Below the fiercely glaring faces they turned to one another, the masks glared as fiercely. With hands spread upon the cheeks of the masks so that the pale smiles, the empty eyes fronted their replicas across the Well like faces in a mirror, the two Isier swayed and panted, waiting. . . .

The hesitating sacrifice dropped into the Well, and the waiting ended.

XIII

THE WELL FLARED HIGH. Up out of it shot enormous bending streamers of white fire, lashing toward the zenith of this golden firmament. But the whirl of the electronic shells intercepted their course, bent them and blew them sidewise as if in the grip of a hurricane, whirled them around and around in intricate, interlacing spiral patterns that seemed to drive the fiery beams faster and faster, endlessly accelerated— What was it Alper had been saying so incoherently, as he stared half dazed into this golden holocaust?

"A cyclotron! Something drives forces around and around the chamber the electrons make!"

And it was true—or an analogy of the truth. The likeness was too clear to miss. Power streamed out of the Well when the sacrifices were fed into it. But the power did not now expend itself outward in invisible waves like a carrier-beam which conveyed energy to the Isier and whatever mysterious receiving-sets and transformers their godlike bodies hid. Power here and now was being confined and driven back upon itself as a cyclotron drives an ion stream faster and faster around wider and wider spirals. What oscillator-force drove it Sawyer could not guess, but the axis it spun on was the same axis the cyclotron uses, pure magnetic force pouring between continua from Earth's Pole itself.

And it was unmistakably clear what purpose this wild spiral served. In a cyclotron the accelerated stream of ions pours at last through an opening that focuses it down to a narrow pencil of tremendously high-energy particles. In the planetary cyclotron of the Hall of Worlds, there was no opening in the artificial chamber the whirling electrons wove. But the pencil of killing energy escaped, none the less. That opening must exist perhaps in a dimensional warp the eye could not follow, but where the beam came out no one

121

could mistake. The deflecting plates that captured it began to light up gloriously.

For now the eyes of the two masks the Isier Goddesses held were filling with solid beams of green fire. Twin rays of it flashed like two drawn blades from each glaring mask—Gorgon glares that crossed in the dazzling air above the well. Their color was the pale green glow of the cathode fluorescent tube, but bright with a terrible brilliance the human gaze could not touch.

And it was doubly terrible to see those pale, serene smiles still fixed upon the masks as the eyes shot out that killing violence. The cyclotron of the worlds whirled more and more furiously as victims dropped down the Well of bubbling flame.

Ring by ring, as the sacrifices dropped, Sawyer was drawn nearer and nearer to the Well. But he forgot his own danger. He forgot the orbit he whirled on, up and over and down again around the nucleus that slowly sucked him in.

All he could see or think of in this moment was the conflict between Goddess and Goddess-elect, fought across the pool where fire instead of water bubbled, and pale beams lashed and clashed like swords more terrible than any blade ever forged.

They were well matched. Endlessly the sweeping slashes caught in midair and hung harmless for a moment before they fell apart and swept treacherously over or under one another at the vulnerable bodies behind the masks.

For to these blades alone the Isier were vulnerable. He saw that now. He saw Nethe suddenly shoot her mask up high above her head at arms' full length, tilt the beams downward and shear across the Goddess's left shoulder with a terrible slash of the green beams from the masks.

The cut bit deep. A dazzling glare sprang out at the impact—the same glare infinitely intensified which had sprung out between Nethe's head and the rock the Sselli hurled at her on the floating island. That protective flare of energy still functioned, then. But it was of no avail, even when stepped up to such blinding power as this, against the slash of the green beams from the masks.

The Goddess reeled. Her mask-guard dropped for a second,

the Gorgon flash from its eyes cutting emptiness. Her black robe parted along an emerald-glowing slash and through it a stream of golden blood poured sluggishly. . . .

Golden blood, Sawyer thought. *Golden blood!* A single, shattering roar went up from the ring of watching angels as that luminous flood gushed over the midnight robe. Nethe screamed, a wild, high, ringing cry of triumph—

There was a jolt that made Sawyer's head swim as he dropped again down the stairsteps of the orbits, this time into the ring only second from the innermost ring of all. He paid no attention. He was only irritated because the jolt made him lose his focus for an instant upon the battle.

For Nethe had overreached herself. She had counted too heavily on dealing a killing stroke, and her mask was too high overhead to parry the Goddess's snake-like twist of recovery. The golden blood still poured, and one black-robed arm hung useless, but with the other hand the Goddess flashed her mask sidewise in a treacherous spiraling sweep. It was an intricate motion, executed with consummate skill, for it seemed to follow exactly and at tremendous speed the spiraling of the power-streams around the cyclotron, to ride with them and perhaps for one brief instant to force more violence out of them through the deflecting-plates which were the eyes of the mask.

She spun her mask to face Nethe's. Eye to eye, face to face, the two Gorgon glares poured their killing energy into one another's smiling faces. Fire flared up from that square, head-on meeting of terrible beams. Nethe's shriek of maniacal fury heralded what had happened even before the blaze faded between the masks. When it cleared, a long, low cry went up from the circling watchers. For one eye of Nethe's mask was blind. The beam had burned out.

With half her fighting strength destroyed, she whirled in redoubled rage at the crippled Goddess, her single beam weaving a net of green fire all about that swaying, parrying figure in black robes. Desperately the Goddess, one-handed but quicker than lightning, wove her own net of defense against the onslaught. And the drain upon the power in the Well grew heavier. . . .

Electrons dropped like snow now out of the innermost

ring. The Well flared, sank, flared again as the lives of the sacrifices fed it briefly, pouring violence into the cyclotron for the Goddesses to wield like flaming swords.

Jolt! Sawyer dropped again. For the penultimate time he dropped. Now he rode the innermost ring, and the next drop would be into the fire.

The fire? He looked down. He looked straight into the Well. And it was bright, bright, bright. . . .

It burned the eye and the brain behind it.

It was not bright at all.

That painful glare transmuted suddenly as he neared it into a beauty that ensnared the very soul. The Well was a wide ring around a flatness and a glassiness like a mirror that reflected only the golden glow of the sky. In the ring glimmered a whirling, spinning, tumbling tumult of—was it molten light, bubbling up from the heart of the world? Bubbling up out of Earth's Pole? Was it a tossing fountain? He could put no name to it. But the tumble and tumult of the fiery pool drew the eye and the mind irresistibly. That tossing motion burned inward to his brain, fusing with it, drawing him down along a chord of his own vision.

He was dropping, dropping. . . .

He wanted to drop. He had to see this thing clearer, closer. Even so near, he thought hazily, the bubbles were still impossible to focus on. What were they? Bubbling liquid metal, cool and bright, like mercury? No, for they were discontinuous. Each tossing, luminous shape was separate, and there was a pattern in their motion. They seemed to weave a dance in and out of the very fabric of his brain, pulling him down into the heart of the beautiful pool, the lovely, tossing dance, the irresistible shimmer and play of enchanting motion. . . .

"Alper!" he shouted suddenly, the sound of his own voice coming back to him deafeningly from the spinning walls of his hexagon.

And Alper responded. In quick, broken bursts the noise of his own blood thundered like deep bells through the chambers of the skull, the hiss of breathing was the steam of a gigantic turbine driving through his head.

With a shuddering breath Sawyer drew back from the

terrible beauty of the pool. He knew what it was, now. Or what it represented. This was a sight no human eye had ever seen before, even in an analogy like the pool.

It was the complex, weaving dance of the nucleus inside the atom. One by one the electrons had drawn inward to hurl themselves into the strong, terrible pull of the protons in the heart of the atom. His turn, now. . . .

But once before, a hurtling electron had paused. Once before he had seen a victim seem to gather himself and resist for a second the merging into that beautiful, fearful dance. Thunder beat strongly in Sawyer's skull and he shut his eyes and let all the revulsion against death that dwells instinct in the mind of man repel the enchantment of the Well.

He dropped no farther.

The Well was an empty mirror in the center of the ring, the mouth of a pool that opened downward on the sun. It yawned for him, but he did not drop. And the brilliance began faintly to haze over, as if a breath had blown across the shining mirror.

Below him the green blades of the Gorgon masks flashed and crossed and hissed upon one another. The murderous strokes wove too fast for the eye to follow. But as he hovered, they seemed to slow. The blades grew paler. The hissing fell softer on the ear.

The Goddess stepped back a pace and looked up. And Nethe, breathing hard, lowered her one-eyed mask and tipped her head back, staring too. Recognition suddenly glowed in her eyes, and she laughed a wild, high gong-note of mirthless greeting.

It was time, and past time, for Sawyer to reach into his pocket, where the Firebird lay. What would happen if he flashed it in her face he did not know but he had no choice now. At any moment he would fall straight into the heart of the boiling Well, and after that there would be no more decisions to make.

He reached for the Firebird—and he could not move.

Some power he could not fight held him as rigid as all the other victims spinning in their electronic shells above the

Well. His mind was free, but his body he could not move by the slightest twitch of a muscle, the least shiver of a finger.

"Alper!" he called desperately. "Step it up! Not too much, but more!"

The continuous low thunder that moved almost unnoticed in his brain grew louder as an express train approaching along a track grows louder, louder, more deafeningly near—

"Hold it!" Sawyer said suddenly. "Keep it there. Wait!"

For from below him, and not far off, another thunder sounded like an externalized echo—the sudden, deep boom of an explosion. In the ring of angels intent upon the duel across the Well, Isier heads turned incredulously toward that sound which might almost have burst within the walls of the Temple itself.

It *was* within the Temple.

It came again, and with it now the crash and the long, sliding rumble of falling walls, just beyond the glow of the golden heavens which wreathed them in.

Then the glass floor rocked beneath the circle of thrones. A crash as of vast glass walls toppling sounded terrifyingly near. The Isier sprang to their feet in one long, undulant wave of rising crowns and tossing robes, whirling outward to face the source of this incredible interruption. For one last instant Sawyer saw them all standing solidly upon emptiness while satellite electrons swung upon their orbits around a sun, and the illusion of circling worlds and gods striding through the void held firm.

Then a great rift opened in the golden heavens. Shards of glass fell shivering through the mist and slid in a great avalanche across the glassy floor. The walls came crashing and great fragments of the falling universe toppled through a gap in the fabric of the heavens, letting appalling glimpses of reality gleam through beyond it.

Through that widening gap a tumult of savages poured across the glass floor toward the waiting angels.

For an instant the Isier stood stunned. Sheer incredulity held them motionless. That the wall *could* be breached must seem the rankest impossibility to their godlike minds, trained for a thousand years to the expectation of submission from all their world. That this holy of holies *could* be violated,

126

that these serpentine savages from the world below *could* be swarming toward them brandishing knives and bellowing their deep, mindless roars, must have a quality of nightmare to the Isier.

So they stood for a moment paralyzed with disbelief.

Then the Goddess screamed to them, and they came alive. The Goddess screamed, and a great, resounding golden chorus of answering shouts replied. Some strange and terrible revulsion seemed to sparkle to life as the assembly of gods swept forward in a wave of ice-colored robes, walking on air, shouting as they surged into combat with the Sselli. Revulsion of like for like, Sawyer thought, remembering the golden blood that was still gushing from the Goddess, and the drop of golden blood that had hung upon his knife-blade when the wound closed in the chest of the Sselli he had stabbed.

Invulnerable race surged forward toward invulnerable race as the savage horde swept across the glass floor toward the gods. For one moment Sawyer saw the blind backward masks of the Isier ranks, facing him and the Well and the battling Goddesses with dispassionate indifference, as if these were the past and of no interest to the race of the gods. Then the Goddess screamed out another cry, and from the charging gods a long, ringing shout of triumph went up, and all through their ranks robed arms rose in a gesture of sheer sweeping joy.

Over their heads with both hands the Isier swept their masks. Now at last the faces which had regarded the past so long and so impassively soared around to face the future. But impassive no longer. Serene no longer. They still smiled their pale curved smiles, but now the smile was terrible, and the eyes above them shot out the twin beams of fiery swords.

Sawyer saw them flame in the very face of the foremost Sselli, already reaching out his long, sinuous arms to grapple with the foremost Isier. The twin rays pierced that thick, scaled chest at the base of the neck, where the sunken head drew down. He saw them go through like light through darkness and emerge in a blurred shimmer at the savage's back.

127

The great, snake-like creature reeled. For an instant the jewel-eyes glared with the same fluorescent greenish glow as the twin beams that pierced him. Then a deep, booming roar burst from him and he hurled himself headlong upon the Isier, golden blood bubbling from his chest.

The Isier tried in vain, with a gesture of fierce repulsion, to fling him away, the mask he held slanting a Gorgon glance of pale violence toward the ceiling. But the savage was not dead. Not yet. With a terrible vitality he writhed his long limbs about the Isier, clawing for the mask. The two struggled titanically, reeled, seemed to revolve in a slow, desperate waltz across the glass floor. The blood of the savage was gushing in a broadening pool at their feet, and Sawyer, watching it spread, realized suddenly that it spread no longer on a flat surface. It was spilling over an unseen verge of glass and falling like golden mist into emptiness. . . .

The transparent platform that held up the thrones was not a solid floor across the abyss. It was a circle floating in haze, held to the golden walls by an intricate pattern of glass bridges that left room for the circling electrons to wheel unhindered over and around and down under the bubbling Well.

Over the edge the Sselli and his Isier enemy toppled, still locked in an embrace of mutual hatred and revulsion. The mask fell with them, raking the misty heavens of the chamber with its pale death-stare of green rays.

As if their fall had broken a spell that held him fascinated, Sawyer came back to life and his own danger. Fiercely he wrenched at the paralysis that held him motionless, for he realized that in another moment or two a burden would be levied upon the Well that not all the sacrifices spinning in their orbits might suffice to bear. This unleashing of every mask at once would demand energy such as the Well might never have been called upon to supply before in all its thousand years.

He focused with desperate intensity upon the sounds of his own private thunder in the cavities of the brain, focused blindly and strove with all his power to break the paralysis . . . And very slightly he moved one hand. Very slightly.

The floating shell under him jolted hard. He opened his

128

eyes and saw in one all-comprehensive flash the battlefield in midair, reeling and staggering with godlike figures and serpentine Sselli gushing golden blood, the two races so like in so many ways that they might almost be the same race seen through distorting lenses in two differing forms—

That thought rang a bell in his memory he had no time to follow. For his cell jolted downward again, and he saw that the drain upon the Well had begun already. The tumble of bright motion below filmed over mistily as every mask drew deep upon the source of all Isier power.

Instantly past Sawyer fell a rain of spinning hexagon-cells, each carrying downward a victim to swell the energy of the Well. Swiftly they dropped, and with each immolation fire seemed to blaze upward from the bubbling ring below. Sawyer set his teeth, called "Alper! More!" and steeled himself to keep his mind awake in the stunning impact of the thunder that followed.

For this last act of immolation, it seemed, must be a voluntary plunge into the Well. The nucleus draws the electron with a summons of mutual irresistible attraction. And if the victim resisted, he could save himself—for awhile. It was why hypnosis had to be part of the initial ceremony. It was why Sawyer could resist, keep his cell suspended against the strong downward pull, so long as his mind kept free. But the irresistible sparkling dance of the patterns below was too powerful to resist forever. . . .

He strained to move his right arm such a little distance, such an impossible distance toward the pocket where the Firebird lay. Was it moving? He could not be sure. He looked down at the terrible panorama below him, seeing the Sselli mowed like serpentine grain before the long green scythes of the Isier, but a grain that would not fall when it was severed. Great pools of shining blood lay suspended as if in empty air on the glass floor, and over the edges of the platform by twos and threes Isier and Sselli pitched screaming, the savages coiling about the bodies of their reapers and dragging them down like dead men still fighting the angels who destroyed them.

It came to Sawyer suddenly why this place of ceremony was called the Hall of the Worlds. That ring of thrones

129

encircling the fiery Well was the symbol in two dimensions of the world of Khom'ad encircling the Under-Shell.

Violently he wrenched at his right arm and felt it move, wrenched again and touched his pocket with the tips of his fingers. He could not be sure that the Firebird would save him. But he was wholly lost if he did nothing, for the pull of the Well was growing stronger. He would not look at it. He would not think of it. But through the bones and the nerves it called him, and in the center of his brain it spun its compelling patterns, until the atoms of his own body felt the summons and grew restless in their paths.

Down about him snowed the summoned sacrifices to feed the Well and keep the green swords flashing. Directly below him he saw Nethe, ignoring the battleground beyond her, stoop and sweep a long sudden slash across the relaxed guard the Goddess had let down to watch her people fighting. . . .

It raked the single hand in which the Goddess held her weapon. The other arm hung limp, and blood dripped down her fingertips and sparkled on the glassy floor. Nethe's one-eyed weapon seared across her knuckles. She whirled and swung her mask up in defense, but slowly, too slowly—

Sawyer's cell jolted once more and hung just above the bubbling Well. The concentrated thunder in his brain was already as strong as he could endure without the danger of blacking out entirely. He could not call on Alper to increase it. He could feel in his own body the treachery of his atomic structure answering the lovely and terrible call of the Well, his nerves accepting what his mind rejected, flesh and bone responding while the will that should control them still said, "Live!" though flesh and bone cried ecstatically, "Die! Die!"

He had to act while he still lived. He had to force his one hand to obedience. He shut his eyes, called to the very limit of endurance upon the tumult in his brain, and—touched the Firebird with his fingertips.

Between thumb and finger he snapped the bright wings open. . . .

STRENGTH POURED through him in a golden flood. The Fire-bird seemed to leap in his hand a little, as if it struggled toward the Well in which its rightful place stood empty, so very near now, waiting for its return. If it went into the Well again the last path to Earth would close forever. And if it did not go in—how long could Sawyer, even with this new strength flooding him, resist the pull of that hypnotic dance?

The choice was not his to make. For as the golden wings spread in his hand, Nethe was loosing her last, her fatal stroke straight into her adversary's face. The newly slashed hand that held the Goddess's mask dropped helpless before Nethe's green-bladed blow, and the Goddess for an instant stood undefended. Nethe's single-eyed weapon swung its Gorgon glare in a long sweep across the Goddess's masked face. And the Goddess cried out in a high, thin scream that echoed inside the Goddess-Mask she wore, and reeled—

Reeled *forward,* toward the Firebird. Her masked eyes burned as she saw it. She stumbled around the edge of the Well, toward Sawyer and the precious thing he held.

Perhaps Nethe felt and saw from the corner of her eyes the sudden spread of sparkling wings above her. Perhaps she only followed the Goddess's lifted gaze. But she whirled as the Goddess's weapon lowered. She too saw the Firebird hovering in Sawyer's hand, no more than head-high above her now. . . .

Did the Firebird's burning power dispel all lesser powers around it? Or did Nethe's sweeping gesture as she whirled dissolve the cell that held Sawyer prisoner above the plat-form? He did not know, but the shining blur of the walls around him vanished and he fell six feet through golden air to land staggering for balance upon that floor of glass above the abyss.

The Firebird was Nethe's for the taking. How could he resist her now? Dazed by the suddenness of his fall, he could only stumble backward away from her and the Well.

Beyond her shoulder he saw the oncoming Goddess, eyes blazing through the jewels of her Goddess-Mask, heard her scream out Nethe's name—saw her swing her weapon shoulder-high with one last, tremendous effort, steadying her slashed hand as she lifted it. . . .

Nethe seemed to whirl in mid-air to meet that final desperate attack. She swung her own weapon around to face the Goddess's, holding it before her like a shield. Face to face and eye to eye the two masks fronted each other, the blazing eye-beams the Goddess wielded smashing the full power of their terrible green blades into the one-eyed face of Nethe's mask.

And Nethe's mask went dead.

She looked down at it, for an instant ludicrously dismayed, holding the useless shield against her with both hands. Then suddenly she laughed, a wild, despairing shriek of ironic merriment. She flung the blind thing from her and twisted like a striking snake straight toward Sawyer and the Firebird.

The impact of her hurtling weight sent him half-stunned to the glass floor. He felt the Firebird snatched from his fingers and heard in his very ear her wild, triumphant scream of unbearable joy as at last, at long last, she closed her hands upon the talisman that could still mean triumph for her.

The scream hung ringing on the air for a moment, full of sound of victory. Then its timbre changed. For the twin beams of the Goddess's deadly mask swept the air above Sawyer's head, and Nethe's scream changed to a long cry of piercing, inhuman pain. . . .

Looking up from the floor, Sawyer saw her towering for one last instant impossibly tall above him, the shining Firebird held high, and the two pale-green beams of the weapon that killed her transfixing her robed body from side to side. She stood there in the moment of her triumph, pinned through by the two green swords, the Firebird pouring useless power through a body no longer able to contain it.

If the Sselli died slowly, the Isier could die more slowly still. It seemed to Sawyer that she stood there an eternity. He saw the inhuman fury, the inhuman despair of her face. He saw it change to implacable determination. She was dead

132

already, and she knew it, as she writhed snake-like toward the Goddess with resolution clear upon her dazzling face. If she could not uphold her own claim to godhood, then no one should win. No one at all. She would bring her whole race crashing with her if she must fall. In no other way could she prove her godhood, but in this way she could and would. . . .

Sawyer saw the flash of her ice-robes streaming, the gush of her luminous blood, the blinding brilliance of the Firebird open and sparkling in her hands, as she hurled herself upon the Goddess. The great blades of the mask still flared between them, but Nethe was beyond the fear of death now. She flung herself forward against the beams that pierced her, straight upon the tall, dark figure of her slayer.

For an instant Sawyer saw them reeling together, in dazzling silhouette against the bubbling fire of the Well behind them. He saw them sway, heard the two voices mingling in a terrible, bell-clear cry. Then together they reeled backward and fell. . . .

The Well received them both.

And with them, flashing and sparkling, fell the Firebird, open-winged, and the end of the race of gods.

Swaying on his feet, dazed and half-blinded by the dazzle of the Well, Sawyer saw them fall. And as they fell, they changed.

Light like vapor seemed to smoke out around them. The molecules of their bodies seemed to disperse and disarrange until only a dance of swarming molecular mist swirled where the two relentlessly interlocked bodies had vanished. And then the mist began to reassemble. . . .

Long, serpentine limbs dawned in that golden haze, condensed into two writhing bodies with the hideous squat heads of the Sselli, and the great, empty, jewel-clear eyes.

He had known it. He had been certain of it, in that well of the mind below the level of awareness. They were the *same*, not two races sprung from one stock but the *same*. The Isier were the Sselli. All the ancient myths of Earth slid dimly through his memory that dealt with the splitting—the fission—of life-forms. Legends of the doppelanger, of possession and exorcism and the divisions between Jekyll and Hyde in all their varied forms.

What unknown link in the bridge between mortal life and atomic energy had the Isier spanned when they first altered themselves into immortal isotopes of their natural form by the lost science of the Well of the Worlds?

No one would ever know, now, but it had been an alteration of deadly danger to themselves, for the instability of the isotope was something which they could not control in this time of crisis. When the Well functioned they had been safe enough, but it was very clear now what peril overtook them when the Well ceased to flow with the energy they required to keep them stable in Isier-form. Energy failed and their bodies flickered down the scale to the next isotopic shape, which was the Sselli. . . .

And the end was not yet. The full circle of the change had not yet closed.

The falling, changing bodies dropped out of sight down the dimension-piercing Well whose other end linked to Earth. There was silence for an instant, while the ring of nuclear patterns tumbled on in its serene, endless dance.

Far off, as it were happening in another world, the battle between Sselli and Isier still raged, a suicidal struggle of a single race pitted against itself by that strange, uncontrollable hatred of like for like. Locked in the relentless embrace of mutual destruction, they still pitched screaming over the rim of the symbolic world toward nothingness, screaming as angels might have screamed who fell over heaven's walls in the War of the Seraphs.

Then, far down in the Well as Sawyer stared after the vanished Goddesses, wings began to flicker, lights began to rise.

Sawyer flung himself flat upon the glass floor, hugged it, strove to be unreal, not there, dead and vanished. For he knew that flicker. He had seen it before, in the Fortuna mine out of which in some incredible way it was now rising, and there was no power in creation that could control it now, with Nethe gone and the summoning symbol with her.

Now the Well was open and uncontrolled, drawing upon

134

the full destruction latent in Earth's poles, and through it, upon other dimensions and other spaces no human mind could grasp.

Up out of the Well a geyser of fountaining violence came pouring. And the geyser was full of the flicker of V-shaped wings and the high, ringing song of the Firebirds, as the whole exploding force of the magnetic fields beyond the Well burst upward into Khom'ad.

In midair the fountain flattened and came showering and soaring down. The living Firebirds swooped in a terrible, scattering swarm over the battle, darting with wings nearly furled, like javelins of fire. Compulsion drove them as strong as the terrible revulsion which locked Isier and Sselli, two by two, in murderous battle whenever they came within arms' reach of one another.

The divided race was recombining, but in a new and violently destructive form. For the Isier isotope had gone through not two, but three alterations before it closed its circle. The Firebirds were the third.

They swooped above the battle, and soared and struck. Wherever they touched the struggling figures below, a fusion took place which the mind could not conceive. Sawyer, hugging the glassy floor, knew he was going mad. No one could watch this happen and not go mad to think of it.

For when the three separate stages of this single basic race fused, there the exploding violence that was geysering up the Well burst out in irresistible fury. Until now, the Isier had been following a circle of change. When energy failed them and they dispersed upon the air in a cloud of molecular mist, they had reassembled through some other-dimensional door upon the world of the Under-'shell, where the Sselli form took shape out of that mist.

But that was not the end. Energy had been lost, and it must somehow be regained. So the Sselli, in their turn, changed too. Again the other-dimensional door opened— but not in this world. It opened upon Earth. It opened at the Pole to which Khom'ad had been indissolubly fixed through the axis of the Well. And avidly into Fortuna poured the glittering Firebirds, which were the third and last unstable isotope of the Isier race. The richly complex uranium with

135

all its potent energy locked inside those heavy structures of electrons had fed the Firebirds until they absorbed enough to whirl them helpless and unremembering back around the cycle into the ice-hall and Khom'ad again. Only Nethe had known what was happening, and all she could do was desperately try to keep the cycle turning without interruption until she could become Goddess and restore the Firebird.

There had always been a safety fuse for the Isier. Originally it had been the Firebird itself, which became non-conductive whenever the other end of the Well touched too powerful an energy-source in the universes beyond Khom'ad. But after the Firebird's theft, the Well no longer poured out the energy the Isier needed, and as they changed into the new and dangerously unstable isotopic form, another, stranger safety-factor came into play, dependent on the low binding forces that hold the heavier elements together. As the atoms of unstable elements may go through a cyclic change—so the matter, the wave-lengths, the form that made up the Isier had been able to pass through a cycle of transmutation.

And it was a safe enough cycle, so long as the three forms did not meet. All the legends that deal with fission between life-forms have the same infallible end. When the divided selves meet, they destroy themselves.

For now the Firebird, the perfect energy-conductor, had charged the inert channel of the Well. It sucked up the energy-forms of the Firebirds from the uranium mine on Earth and drew them inexorably back to Khom'ad to complete the fatal isotopic interlocking.

This time it was not a circle but a spiral they followed, the same suicidal spiral that begins with uranium 238 and whirls so swiftly through the instability of neptunium to plutonium and back to uranium again, but 235 this time, and—fissionable. In critical mass—it explodes.

Within the Well there sprang into visibility the whirling glimpse of a planet, falling, spinning, diminishing as the bond between Earth and Khom'ad snapped and the two worlds swept apart in space, and then irrevocably were parted by the wall between two kinds of space, two dimensions that could never touch except through the adaptive link of the Well itself.

The Well opened into a blackness beyond space and time.

But up from it still poured the fountain of the Firebirds, bringing the last necessary factor into the equation. The cyclotron of the planet shuddered under the impact of this titanic energy, and—

The new isotope formed. The utterly new element that was Isier, Sselli, and Firebird combined into critical mass.

One instant Sawyer saw them stand fused and locked into three inter-dissolving figures wherever the merging struck them, three and yet impossibly one. Serpentine savage and shining demigod a monad together, with winged fire lifting from the shoulders of each unbelievable golden figure, they stood frozen.

This was Satan before the Fall, Sawyer thought insanely, his face pressed to the transparent floor that did not stop his seeing. Tremendous shining figures, part serpent, part angel, winged with fire that made the very mind go blind with its brilliance.

One instant they stood godlike in space, locked in a frozen moment of conflict. Then the geyser of exploding violence burst outward, like the cloud that stood first over Almagordo. Terribly it hung above the hollow world of Khom'ad— hung and spread.

It spread through directions the mind could not follow, nor the eye. The Firebird that could irresistibly conduct all energies drank now the energies of the Isiers' death. The demigods who, in making themselves immortal, had extended into—into elsewhere, now saw the cloud of their destruction burst *elsewhere* and roll in great, blinding billows of violence *elsewhere*, while the flesh of the gods went up together in the fires of heaven.

Only the echoes of gigantic thunder rolled through the vast and empty sanctum as rifted space healed itself after the passing of the gods. And the axis upon which all their power had turned was the Well of the Worlds no longer.

Dead, empty, burned-out blankness, the Well lay charred upon the glassy floor. Sawyer's dazzled eyes still held the after-image of its final blaze as it died, and that glitter upon

137

his eyelids was the last thing he saw as all memory failed him.

Thunder in his head shocked him to life. He stood on glass, above golden emptiness. He had been standing here a long time, facing a Mask.

He could not remember clearly.

But a masked figure was coming toward him slowly through the breach in the glass wall where a thousand years ago, it seemed to him, he had watched the Sselli pouring. He knew now why he stood motionless, and what he awaited.

From beyond the broken wall a murmur and a rising chorus of men's voices was beginning to echo higher and higher in a crescendo of triumph. He heard bells far off begin to swing, not in alarm now but in paeans of thanksgiving.

Only here inside the sanctum of the vanished gods was it not yet time for triumph. Peace had not yet come here. Everywhere else upon the hollow world it dwelt, but a masked man walked slowly toward Sawyer, and with him came death.

But he came unsteadily, upon failing legs. For the last energy of the Firebird was beginning to flicker out in Alper's ponderous body.

Ten feet away he paused, braced himself. It was strange, Sawyer thought, to be looking at an Isier mask out of whose eyes no streams of killing violence poured. Alper's small grey eyes gazed dully instead from the empty sockets of the Isier-face; he must have picked it up from the battlefield of Armageddon, as he came.

"It's gone," he said, *"You let the Firebird go!"*

"Earth's gone too," Sawyer heard his own voice answer. He drew a deep, dazed breath. "There's no way back. Killing me won't help. We can live—I suppose—in Khom'ad—"

"Alper!" a voice called. "Alper, wait!" Zatri's portly, masked figure was scrambling through the avalanche of shattered glass toward them, the echoes of his voice rolling under the great vault. Zatri too still wore his mask. What had been happening outside while the Armageddon of the Isier went on Sawyer did not even wonder. If Alper and the Khom had worked together during the crisis in masked communication,

138

it made no difference now. There was still one last battle to be fought, and no one could help Sawyer but himself.

"Live here?" Alper said bitterly. "Without the Firebird? How long would I last? You've got time! You'll find some damned plodding job andd work at it all your life. You'll marry. You'll raise a family. But what about me? How can I *rule—*"

"You can't," Sawyer said calmly. "You're through ruling. There are jobs here you could do well, but ruling isn't one of them."

"Alper!" Zatri shouted. "Wait!"

"Wait?" Alper snarled in his mask. "What for? So you can noose me again? Oh no!" He sprang toward Sawyer, his clenched fists lifting. "You threw away the Firebird! Without it I'll die. I'll die!" The smiling mask roared suddenly, "But you'll die first!"

The fists unfolded. The right hand dropped toward that pocket where the transceiver control lay.

Knowing he was too late, still Sawyer leaped.

The turbulent lightnings crashed through his brain, mounted to a deadly crescendo. Now it was his own skull that was the chamber of a cyclotron, driving violence faster and faster, louder and louder as he stumbled blindly toward the serenely smiling mask. . . .

His hands flew up to hold his skull together, and he knew dimly that he too wore a mask. He had wholly forgotten that. It had not even seemed strange to him that he understood Zatri's words. Zatri—

Dimly he saw Zatri doing something very strange. Zatri too was clasping his temples with both hands, and in the moment Sawyer's gaze touched him the old man tore off his mask and sent it clashing and rolling across the glass floor. His face was convulsed with surprise and pain as he stared from Sawyer to Alper.

All of it happened between two halves of the same second, while Sawyer leaped toward the man who was doing his best to split his skull in two. In the middle of the leap, in the middle of the second, as he saw Zatri's uncovered face, Sawyer quite suddenly realized the truth. He laughed with

139

a choke of triumph, and in mid-air ripped off the mask he wore—

Then he struck Alper and the old man went down, hand still pressing the control. But this time Sawyer wanted it pressed. For he knew why Zatri had torn off the mask, and he knew what was happening in Alper's own skull.

Alper made one useless guesture toward his own mask in the instant before Sawyer struck him. For he too had realized in the same instant, what was wrong.

The masks were transceivers too, in their own strange way. They were transmitters of sound and energy-waves, creating their own carrier-beams. And they were tremendously powerful amplifiers. Sight and sound perceived through them were the sights and sounds a god might know, vivider than human senses ever receive. And the ultra-sonic vibrations that roared now through Sawyer's skull were roaring many times magnified through Alper's—while he wore his mask!

Sawyer's impact rolled the old man over on the floor, and Sawyer with one hand pressed the back of Alper's head hard to hold his masked face down upon the glass, fixing the mask in place. With the other hand he groped for Alper's on the transceiver control, found it, closed hard. . . .

Alper *screamed.*

Under Sawyer's grip his fingers fumbled wildly at the control. Thunder beat blindingly in both heads alike, deafening Sawyer, dazing him, but roaring with killing force through Alper's head behind the mask. Alper must be hearing ten times the fury of lightning and thunder that pounded through Sawyer's skull.

Now Alper's only thought was to release the pressure upon the control, to stop that thunder in Sawyer's head and the infinitely worse vibrations of his own. But Sawyer's grip would not let go. Stunned and dizzy, he crushed the old man's hand still harder upon the controls. There was one hope for him now and only one. If Alper could find the hidden release which Sawyer could not find, and spring it before this thunder killed them both. . . .

If Alper died before he found it, Sawyer was doomed too. For while the transceiver linked them, Alper's death meant Sawyer's.

Desperately the old man's fingers fumbled at the control. Sawyer dared not let go fully, but he released the pressure a little—just a little—and the fingers under his twisted purposefully at the disc they clasped. . . .

Then, without any warning at all, it was over.

Dazed by the suddenness of his release, by the echoing silences in his own brain, Sawyer crouched over the old man's body and heard something tinkle on the glass beside him without at first realizing what it was. His dulled eyes saw it roll—a little disc tiny as an aspirin tablet, shining metal, curved inward on the underside—

The transceiver.

Hardly daring to believe it, he released Alper with one hand and pressed his palm to his head. It was gone. He was free.

Very slowly, as Sawyer's hands released him, Alper rolled sidewise on the floor, straightened and was still. The heavy head rolled back until the Isier mask stared up at Sawyer with its eternal, serene smile. The grey eyes behind it were no less empty than the mask, staring up into Sawyer's face and seeing nothing at all. Age had been Alper's terror— and he would never be older now.

After what seemed a long, long time, Sawyer lifted his gaze from the dead man's.

Zatri was coming toward him across the glass floor. Beyond him, by the broken wall, Klai stood watching. She lifted an unsteady hand when her eyes met Sawyer's, and he smiled without moving. He could not move. He was too tired.

But it was all over now. He glanced sidewise once, for the last time, at the ruined Well that was nothing but fused metal now. Beyond it, beyond dimensions of space and time, his own lost world spun eternally severed from Khom'ad. That was irrevocable. He had done the best he could. He had done his job.

An infinity away through the vastness of other-space, someone in an office in Toronto would write "Closed" across a folder and file it in a steel cabinet. Sawyer shook his head hard. Now there was only Khom'ad. There could be a good life on Khom'ad too—but that was up to him.

He turned toward Klai, waiting in the portal. Moving heavily, he got to his feet.

A man can find a job in any world. He knew he would not forget Earth. Wryly he thought that when he drank too much he would talk of it. If there was liquor on Khom'ad, he would certainly drink too much, at first—and babble, he told himself—of green fields. There would be at least one time more when Earth came back to his thoughts and his speech more vividly than when he had dwelt on Earth— the last time a man ever speaks of anything at all.

But he was young, now. He had a long life ahead of him. It could be good, if he made it good.

The serenely smiling mask on Alper's face watched him walking steadily over the swimming golden void toward Zatri, and toward Klai.

The cream of the year's science-fiction stories is in this new Ace anthology:

WORLD'S BEST SCIENCE FICTION: 1965

EDITED BY
DONALD A. WOLLHEIM & TERRY CARR